This is a work of fiction. Names, characters, universes, satirical corporate amalgams, and climate change either are products of the author's cynical imagination or are used fictitiously. Any resemblance to actual events or locales or persons or artificial intelligences or money-grubbers, living or dead or immortal, is entirely coincidental.

ISBN : 978 1 7381571 4 3

Douglas Gets A Suicide

A Novella

By

K.R. Carnegie

This one is for my brothers,
the taller one and the tallest one,
and all the others by choice.

Chapter One
Douglas Has an Idea

"I think I might go for a suicide today," Douglas remarked as he buttered his stale morning toast on a day not so far away from now. Douglas loved breakfast.

"Mmm-hmm," replied his partner, not looking up from their phone. Douglas frowned.

"Did you even hear me?" asked Douglas in a tight voice, putting the half-buttered toast down on his plate, his voice slathered like his buttery bread, only with weariness instead of synthetic fat.

"What? Yes, yes, of course I did," his partner replied, a chime on their phone eliciting a slight smirk on their wrinkled, oily face. "You're heading up to Toronto to visit the Placement Office today. You better hurry- the TV says it's going to rain today. Good luck with that."

Douglas sighed and leaned back in his chair. Even sitting down, he looked down on them, his tall frame in stark contrast to their petiteness and lightness. He ran his hand through his brown-going-grey hair as he looked around the kitchen for the right words. Talking to his partner was a delicate affair, and he needed the right words for this situation. The early morning light struggled to shine through the crooked, dirty window into their kitchen, weak beams ushered around the room by motes of dust dancing between the shifting shadows. The paint was peeling along the moulding, and some black fuzzy furrows of dirt (or more likely mold) creeped from each crack along the countertop. A draft creeped through the askew window as he watched a skeletal tree dancing in the warm morning wind.

"Yes, yes I said that," said Douglas exasperated, "The second part."

"Second part? What second part? You didn't say a second part, dummy." They offered a smile that struck Douglas as exceedingly lupine, like a wolf wearing lipstick.

Douglas felt an emptiness in his stomach and took a tepid bite of his terribly unsatisfying toast. "I was thinking of going to the AAVR today."

That got his partner's attention.

"The Moodmen?" They asked, the scorn hidden in their voice but not on their face, "Whatever for?"

"Well," whispered Douglas, "I was thinking of going for a suicide."

His partner's face turned crimson, the first warning sign. Douglas didn't notice, or perhaps he just chose not to notice. In any case, it was a mistake. Just one of many Douglas would make throughout the day.

"Is that so," they said tightly, staring at Douglas, their hand clutching the phone so hard the plastiglass screen strained under the pressure.

"Yes," he continued, just the slightest bit more confidently, "I was thinking of going after I go to the PO. Brian- you know, Peter's husband- he said they're having a Valentine's Day special and so..."

Here came the interruption, which Douglas had anticipated. "Do you really think we have the money for that?"

Douglas steeled himself. He promised himself he wasn't going to lose the argument this time.

"It's not a question of money, love-"

“Not about money! Everything is about money!”

Douglas kept going, knowing if he stopped the argument was over for him. “I still have my benefits from that half-day placement at the maintenance depot- they don’t stop them until April. They’ll cover half the cost. And with the special-”

His partner snorted, looking back down at their phone, swiping through pictures of smiling faces in tropical climates. “Oh, and where is the other half coming from? The Moodmen don’t take credit, and you’re poor as shit. UBI won’t pay for you to play dead. The answer is NO.”

Douglas arched an eyebrow and wiped his sweaty palms on his plastisheath slacks underneath the table. “No?” He repeated in a tremulous voice.

“Did I stutter?” They shot back acidly. They placed their phone delicately on the table, with a motion that reminded Douglas of a mantis with slow and calculated movements. Douglas, desperately trying to maintain his courage, tried to ignore the coiling and tense body language. “No. We don’t have the money. You can’t go to the Moodmen,” was said with an air of sick sweetness, a tone of ‘keep pushing and find out what happens’ unmistakable.

Douglas tried to steady his breathing, his empty stomach turning sour. “If you, uh, didn’t play the lottery this month-”

The whirling dish barely missed his head, the impromptu missile impacting the far wall and doing nothing to improve the peeling paint. “NO LOTTO!?!?” they exploded, “Not play my games? ARE YOU SERIOUS?”

“Honey,” pleaded Douglas, holding up his hands, palms outward.

“DON’T HONEY ME! I CAN’T BELIEVE HOW SELFISH YOU ARE!”

“Please, just calm down.” He trembled.

“The lottery is the only Jobs damn thing I look forward to!”

“I know!”

“Did I complain when you wanted to move out of Peche? Leaving everything behind?”

“No, no of course you didn’t-”

“But you promised I would still get to play the lotto!”

“Moving out here means we could do both-”

“And you want to take it away! The only thing I look forward to!”

“No, it’s not that,” stuttered Douglas.

"You don't care about me at all."

"I do! I won't go to the Moodmen! I swear!"

His partner sniffled, placing their fork down on the table. "I'm sorry," they said between sobs.

Douglas sprang up and moved around the table, draping his arm around his partner. "No! No, honey, it's me who is sorry. It was just an idea- forget I even mentioned it!"

His partner's hand creeped out and turned their phone off just as it dinged with an incoming message, flipping it face-side down. "I'm sorry about the plate... I just worry about you so much, that you make me lose my mind..."

"Hush, love," whispered Douglas as he tried to still his shaking hands, "It was my fault. No more talk of suicide. Forget I said anything."

Douglas' partner sniffled and coughed, their eyes bright and shining. "You better hurry. Weather Disney says its going to rain- you might want to bring the emergency flares."

The sun was threatening from behind the eastern horizon, while the rain remained hidden in a long-off creeping darkness from the west.

Douglas' shoes squeaked as he walked down the empty crumbling driveway of his home in the pre-dawn heat. It had been at least three decades since it had been re-tarred, a fact of which Douglas was ignorant. If he had ever owned a car, he might have thought of its state more often. Instead, if he thought of the driveway at all, it was in terms of being an eyesore. At least in that respect it was in very good company.

His house was a small pre-war backsplit, built back before the modern arcologies replaced traditional housing. In the old days it would have been condemned-nowadays it was a very affordable fixer-upper. Back then, affordable would have meant a couple decades salary. Nowadays, affordable meant free. Back then, Douglas would have been considered a squatter. Nowadays, Douglas would most definitely be considered a squatter. Some things never change.

Douglas did not consider himself a squatter, not that the word had much weight in this modern era. The houses in this area had been hit hard in the old war, and even harder during the insurrections that followed. Its not like anyone else wanted to live on an ancient wasteland battlefield. Well, almost no one wanted to.

Hopping over a gaping sinkhole that had long ago been a sewer drain, Douglas pulled his ancient and perpetually mended windbreaker tightly around his sleek frame. The draping sleeves flapped like pennants from his spindly arms, a threadbare patch proclaiming the 2046 NFL world champion Hamilton Steelers in faded glory on the back. The bright yellows of his jacket were no longer all that yellow, but the colour still stood out against the dour surrounding of his neighborhood.

Only a quarter of the lots still had houses on them. Of those houses, only half were fit for habitation. The other half were half-burnt husks with eyes of shattered glass, board-and-batten walls vandalized into tattooed faces of neon spray paint gang tags, mouths nailed shut with plywood stamped in red paint. Some were of lesser quality than even those abandoned corpses- quite a few were open graves of cracked concrete, holes filled with cat-sized rats squirming among trash and brackish water. “Condemned,” read red-painted warnings, and for the thousandth time, Douglas made it into a song as he walked along. “Condemned… condemning damn… oooo….”

Douglas jumped with a start as a pack of dogs sprang from a nearby lot of overgrown cedars, half a dozen snarling mongrels chasing an emaciated squirrel. Even with the pack of mutts running at full speed Douglas could count their jutting ribs. One of the dogs, an old somewhat-curly half-hairless shepherd, stopped slightly to snarl at him before following after his pack. The old collar around it's scraggly neck was weathered and frayed while its hind was a patchwork of messily healed scars. Douglas wondered what his one-time master had called him.

"Good morning, Dougy!"

The greeting startled Douglas more than the dogs had, even though he should have been expecting it. It was a rare morning when he could get from his home to the bus stop without being accosted by the one and only neighbour also eke-ing out a living on this decrepit street.

"Ah, yes, good morning," stammered Douglas, "How are you today, Billy?"

The smell of bourbon heralded Douglas' neighbour before he had closed half the distance between them, bounding towards him from his well fortified porch. His hair was a greasy black of twisted wires that had not seen a barber in many years. A thin whip in a billowing trench coat with no undershirt, Bill Cronkwright was a wiry man of later years with corded muscles and a fennec smile that made Douglas think of a cartoon character from the old days when he was a child. In all of the dozen years Douglas had known him, he had never stepped foot in the man's home. A large steel door provided the only entrance to Bill's Lair of Mystery, thick sheets of plywood with thin black slits bordering every square inch of the home. Douglas had met a few of his "children", each one bearing no resemblance in the slightest to their supposed father. He eyed the slits cautiously. Doug knew for a fact that despite knowing Billy for more than a decade (he was pretty sure he was the only person Bill considered a friend, and quite possibly the only person he personally knew outside of his 'family') that their unseen eyes and weapons were firmly trained and fixed on him.

"How goes it, my friend!" Bill had a rough voice, tinged with an effortless joviality that rarely reached his eyes.

"Oh, can't complain, Billy," answered Douglas, not stopping as he walked past the house, and if anything, slightly increasing his pace.

Bill fell in step alongside him. "That's good, that's good," he nodded, "Ain't nobody gonna listen anyways, right?" He laughed.

"True enough, true enough."

"Where ya heading today, brother?"

Douglas sighed. "Time for my scheduled yearly beatdown."

Bill laughed. “The PO, eh? I swear to god, Doug, you’re the only person living outside the Arcos still on the dole. You’ll have to tell me again sometime how you pulled that one off. I’ve told you so many times, brother, it’s a waste of fucking time. Just 401 ‘em and come work for me! The States ain’t looked for off-liners in years. They wouldn’t even have the money to bother if they managed to give a fuck about peeps like me.”

“Can’t do that,” said Douglas, only slightly regretfully. “Won’t be able to play the lotto if we go offline.” Douglas grimaced, thinking of the fight- no, the cataclysm- with his partner that would ensue if he went off-line. That set Bill to a fit of laughter so fierce he doubled over and had to skip a couple of steps to catch back up.

“The fucking lotto? That’s what’s stopping you? Are you mad, Dougy?”

“It’s for the missus,” he muttered.

Bill’s laughter petered out. “Ah, of course. The missus.” He coughed, clearing his throat. “Ya know, Dougy, you could make good money with me. I could always use another set of hands on my midnight runs, if you know what I mean.”

Doug entertained the thought for half a second longer than he usually did. "I know, Billy. I appreciate the offer. Can't risk it. I need to stay good with the PO."

"Fuck the PO," spat Bill scornfully, "There's plenty of jobs to be had out here in the wreckage, y'know. Y'know- I haven't even owned a smartphone in years?"

"You may have mentioned it once or twice."

"Trust me, Dougy, life is better my way. No damn phone, no damn internet. No damn PO or taxes. No damn lotto. No one telling you there's no god damn jobs. No damn wi-"

"Did you want something, Billy?" He was pretty sure what his neighbour was about to say and had learned it was better to cut his wily neighbour off before he went down that road.

Bill looked slightly hurt. "What? Do I need a reason to be neighbourly?" He side-stepped an ancient black plastic bag of deflated trash. It lied forlornly on the curb in front of a plasti-crete lot of twisted shopping carts. Douglas had passed by it at least a thousand times on his way to the bus, and often wondered what was in it. He would never, ever touch it despite his curiosity. He had taken to calling it Burt a few years back, a personification he had kept to himself.

Douglas went flush. "Sorry, sorry Billy, I'm just... I'm just in a mood today."

Bill waved a hand dismissively. "No apology necessary, I get it, I get it, I have bad days too."

Douglas was familiar with this prompt. Douglas had become adept at recognizing when someone wanted to talk about themselves. "Is that so? What's a bad day for Billy Cronkwright?"

He whistled low as he stretched out his spine, his arms like straight bars of twisted iron pushing two clenched fists into his pockets, stretching the trench coat and popping a few stitches. "Fuck brother, where do I begin? A bad day is when Mandy and BJ get into it." A flock of crows cawed overhead. Douglas face screwed up.

"Mandy? BJ?"

Billy shot him a comically exaggerated look of incredulity. "Mandy! BJ! You met them! Mandy with the, the pigtails. And BJ with the black market low jack."

"Oh," nodded Douglas, the image of the sweet girl with crooked teeth and the young man with the hack job brain implant, "Yes, of course."

"Yah, you know them," nodded Billy energetically, satisfied, "Like I was saying, when they get into it, hoo-boy, now that's a bad day for ole' Billy."

“They fight often?”

“Nah,” denied Billy, “I put ‘em straight when they get out of line.”

Douglas didn’t know what that exactly meant and didn’t want to. He had never had children and did not understand them a great deal. They walked on a few meters in silence, something that Billy could never tolerate for very long.

“Weather is trash, ain’t it? Weather-Disney says it might even snow today! Can you believe it?”

“No.” Douglas looked up at the sky, overcast and dreary. “It hasn’t snowed here in over twenty years.”

Bill nodded. “Exactly. Fakes news, right? Remember how it used to be? I’d love to show my little ones snow. Build a snowman, throw some snowballs. Like when we were kids, eh?”

“Ah, yes. I remember.” Doug’s thoughts turned back to suicide. “You could always take them to the Moodmen.”

“Excuse me?” asked Billy, confused.

“Your kids. If they’re fighting.”

Anger flashed across Bill’s face. “Ha. Good one.”

Douglas had anticipated this response. He shrugged. “I’m just saying.”

“Wait.”

Douglas stopped, turning around. Bill stood in the middle of the road, an expression halfway between amusement and scorn painted on his face. A murder of crows had settled a few paces behind him, pecking over a dried-out husk of greyish hair and sun-bleached bone. A loud honking echoed from somewhere behind him, carrying over from the main road, as a swarm of geese passed by. The crows barely looked at the geese, acknowledging them with a modicum of casual disdain. Douglas stood staring at him, pressing his nails into the palm, hidden by his white-knuckled closed fist. After a pregnant pause, Douglas grunted in frustration.

"What, Billy? I have places to be. Spit it out."

Billy scoffed. "Oh, you have to be at the PO? Fuck off."

"Spit it out!"

Billy squinted. "You're thinking of going. Aren't you?"

"Going where? The PO?"

"Don't be daft. The Moodmen!"

Douglas blushed. "So? What if I am?"

Billy threw his hands up and frantically paced in a circle. "So what? So what!" He abruptly changed direction and marched up into Douglas' face, causing him to panic and lose his footing for a moment. He knew, or at least guessed, that Bill was harmless. Mostly. It still set his nerves on edge to have someone so close up in his personal space.

"The fucking Moodmen," continued Billy, shaking his head, "I thought you were smarter than that, Dougy. Don't you know what those guys do to you?"

"Well, yah. It's in the name."

"Moodmen? They fuck more than your mood-"

"No," interjected Douglas, more tersely and more vocally than he had intended, "the actual name. The AAVR."

Bill looked at him skeptically. Douglas was not surprised.

"The AAVR," he repeated, slowly and annunciating each letter, "The Attitude Adjustment Virtual Reality."

Bill shook his head angrily. "I knew that!"

Douglas ignored him, turning around and continuing along his path. He thought for a moment that Billy would follow, but after a second he could hear his retreating footsteps. He rarely followed after a disagreement. The crows took flight in an indigent chorus as the eccentric man marched back to his redoubt, his fortress of lumber, steel and trash. Douglas knew for a fact he would see him on his return home. Some people in life you could just depend on.

Chapter Two
You Don't Talk on Bus

The bus stop was on a wide two-lane street running adjacent to his neighbourhood. There had been a bus shelter once, but that had disappeared quite a few years ago in one of the more intense summer storms. The bench, having been bolted into the concrete sometime in the distant past, remained. It was a thick iron seat, a zebra with rusty red stripes. It could sit three people. Douglas, despite being an immense fan of seats in general, never sat on it, and therefore it remained unoccupied every time Doug had to catch the Bus.

The next nearest bus stop was so far away it might as well have been on Mars. Bus's service budget had been cut, and cut, and cut again with each passing year as fewer and fewer people needed to travel outside. It made conditions on Bus less pleasant as the years wore on but considering it hadn't been great to begin with it mattered little to Douglas.

Bus was usually late. This didn't bother Douglas anymore. He had written letters to the Upper Great Lakes Transit Authority once upon a time, eloquently laying out the faults he perceived in the local public transit as well as an itemized list of chronological steps that he had developed to increase efficiency and reduce costs. He never heard back, and as far as he could tell, his suggestions had never been implemented. He said it didn't bother him but shortly after, once he had admitted to himself that his thoughtful plan was not going to get any type of response, he had stopped sitting on the bench. He still dreamed of sitting on Bus. He considered adding seats to Bus the best of his suggestions.

The bus stop was on a slight rise, offering a splendid if somewhat depressing vista to the north. The current state of the once 'Great' lake was a brown-grey ribbon on the northeastern horizon beyond the sands and rocks of the old lakebed. The far end of the great city could be easily seen from across the wasteland, an unending line of enormous buildings jutting up like jagged fangs spanning the entire length of the far, far shore. Smudges of black smog curled around the arcologies, the great city-towers of the future, like a sinister lower lip baring it's teeth. On this side of the old lake, chequered fields of concrete veined with long erratic lines of wild grasses spread before him. Old seeds stubborn and tough had pierced through their concrete cairns, nourished by the old, rich soil underneath. Douglas couldn't remember why these cold stone meadows were here. He might have heard of a parking lot once upon a time, but the word eluded him now.

The sun was climbing a quarter of the way into the sky before the keening whir of Bus came screaming in from the west. He shielded his eyes from the reflected glare of the rising sun off the metal carapace of the gigantic electric vehicle. It was working its way up the sharp incline towards Douglas when a pack of crows- perhaps the ones from before, perhaps not- decided to cut across the highway. The bus slowed not an inch. A couple of crows proved a little too slow, and the resulting impact couldn't be discerned from this distance, but Douglas assumed it was quick and painful.

Douglas knew that if he jumped in front of the bus- it would never happen, Douglas was afraid of pain- it would stop anyway before impact. The driver had reflexes that would put a bondo-cat to shame, and there had been no external public transit fatalities in a very long time. The UGLTA was very, very proud of its drivers, having determined that the cost of the advanced drivers far outweighed the estimated penalty payment to bereaved families.

It took another minute for the bus to reach Douglas' stop. The gargantuan vehicle lurched to an abrupt stop, rocking on it's eighteen pairs of man-sized, wide-track wheels. It slouched forward a good two metres before rolling back and settling down. An ear-splitting pneumatic hiss scared a couple of close-by gliding rats as an anticipated blast of hot air scalded Douglas' face and Bus lowered itself closer to the ground. The sheer metal wall in front of him, nearly three stories high, was in desperate need of a wash. Innumerable rainbow streaks of various matter splattered across the bus, resulting in a somewhat pleasing mural reminiscent of a Jackson Pollack painting. A perfectly clean square about the size of a bathroom window was directly in front of him. After a moment a smiling cartoonish face of a moustachioed man with a blue cap emblazoned with the UGLTA logo bloomed into existence on the pristine metallic surface.

"Good day... Douglas!" The disembodied head had a unique Upper New York accent, the "O"s in good sounding like a "U" and the "O" in his name sounding more like an "A".

"Hello, Bus," replied Douglas tonelessly.

The face stayed silent for an awkward pause before resuming in the same cheerful manner.

"Where are we going today, friend?"

"The PO."

The smile didn't drop from Bus' face, but all movement ceased for a moment while the AI parsed his answer.

"I do apologize, Douglas!" Bus sounded contrite, but the face had not changed from the leering grin. "I don't recognize that location!"

Douglas sighed. "Sorry, Bus. Downtown. Toronto. The Placement Office."

The reply came much quicker this time. "I'd be happy to take you to... The Placement Office, located in... Toronto. The cost of the ride will be charged to your Personal Ident Number. Do you accept?"

"Yes."

"Thank you, Douglas!" His wrist vibrated as his PIN implant acknowledged the debit to his personal account. "Your spot is level 3, space 389. Thank you for riding with the UGLTA!" The insufferably chipper face of Bus vanished in a blink, as heretofore invisible seams in the grey wall appeared. The door swung up and lifted in front of him like a spread wing, nearly knocking Douglas in the chin before he hopped back. A cool blast of stale, plastic air took his breath away momentarily before he stepped onto the elevator, leaving the rising heat of the day blissfully behind. The sweat on his neck sent a tingle up his spine as he acclimatized to the tight confines of the lift.

The elevator was a tight fit, even for a fairly skinny man like Douglas. The dull industrial grey plastic tube disappeared as it began to ascend. In its place was a virtual display, a panoramic view of Old Niagara Falls, in the days long before. Douglas smiled slightly. He imagined himself a great bird high above the river. A wide and tall column of water vapour erupted from the foot of the falls, glistening in the light like a benign volcano, enveloping the nearby buildings. The tops of the quaint skyscrapers looked like castles in the sky, nestled between clouds. He glided between the old nation of Canada and the older, smaller United States of America, soaring on the updrafts from the thunderous roar of the lost wonder of the world. A needle tower with a large disc was nearby, a tower that Douglas thought looked similar to the American Express Patriot Tower in the heart of the city, but much smaller in height. Two ferries bounced along the choppy waves far below. From this height they looked like a child's bathtub toys.

There were no tenements, no towering arcologies blotting the horizon. There were no scorched or blown out tanks. No craters. No pools of poison collecting in long abandoned trenches. No scavenger ambushes, no packs of roaming dogs or rats or spiders. No unexploded warheads just waiting for the right gust of wind, or shift of land, or weather a tad too powerful; no tools of destruction waiting for any chance to fulfil their purpose, their raison d'etre. No beasts of war trampling their way north. No concrete mausoleums the size of city blocks filled with the unknown dead. No transformers and batteries and generators and turbines and the millions of kilometres of snaking black and steel cable connecting it all. No monsters.

"No despair," whispered Douglas aloud, barely audible. He wiped his face.

The pleasant illusion dissolved into a million dim snowflakes. Douglas' smile vanished. The stark logo of the UGLTA replaced it as a chime sounded and the door opened to the dim space of the bus's third floor. The stale air from before was now mixed with the scent of unwashed humanity, a cloying sour smell that stirred memories of another life.

Douglas stepped forward and turned, walking back among the rows of standing men, women and children. The bus itself was the size of a school gymnasium, divided into three floors. Each floor was further divided into one hundred sections denoted by highly reflective yellow paint on the floor, which still remained surprisingly visible through years of encrusted grime and the passengers' long shadows. Glaring spotlights broadcasting from hanging monitors illuminated the passengers faces; every wrinkle, scar, deformity, mutation and lesion visible in the stark harsh light; disembodied heads floating above blackness with jaundiced veins. Nearly all of the faces were downturned, eyes fixed on glowing phones.

His shoes squelched as he overcame the omnipresent stickiness of the centre aisle way. As he approached his row, a frazzled looking woman with greasy red hair typed furiously on the device clutched in her hand as a small child curled around her legs. The child was a girl of no more than five by the looks of it, but that could be deceiving in certain circumstances. It was doubtful judging by their clothes (and the fact that they were riding Bus) that this was such a circumstance. Rejuve treatment was fiscally out of reach for most people who rode the bus. Douglas tried to smile at the little one as he passed, and the child shrank back behind her mother's legs. Douglas decided that she was just shy instead of fearful. It made him feel better.

"Excuse me, excuse me, pardon me," he murmured as he squeezed into his row and space. He ignored the scowls, wondering if they had expected him to jump over their heads to get to his spot. He found his assigned number, the 89 looking more like 30 given the state of the floor. His shoulders slouched as he exhaled, settling into a posture that just might not kill his back during the half an hour or so ride. Douglas wasn't that hopeful, but he still felt the need to try. Another chime, and Bus' beaming face materialized on the monitors.

"Hello passengers!"

A smattering of half-hearted 'hi, bus' returned the vehicle's greeting, as well as one vehement 'fuck you' filtering up from the floor below them.

"Now, now, passenger," chided Bus good-naturedly, "Profanity is not tolerated on any and all UGLTA conveyances.

"We are currently heading west on the Great Victory Way- non-stop to Downtown. The weather today is expected to be at red level. Outside temperature is currently 81, with an expected daytime high of 121. Remember your sunblock! We also have a special weather warning in effect- severe rainfall is expected in the evening hours. Please folks, be safe! We will arrive at Grand Union Station around approximately 9:45 am. From your friends at UGTLA, thank you for riding Bus!"

The face went away again. Douglas liked to imagine that Bus had a little room hidden somewhere on the actual, physical bus. He liked to imagine that when he wasn't gleefully informing his passengers of the weather or chiding them gently for boorish behaviour, he nestled down in a recliner and cracked a beer. He liked to imagine Bus hated every one of them, and that his smile would be gone, and he would watch his passengers from his cyber-lair and curse each one of them to hell. He liked to imagine he was real, with real dreams and real purpose outside of public transportation.

The truth was that Bus was, in the strictest sense of reality, a tiny silicon wafer no bigger than a grain of rice. On that well-shielded, well-protected chip lived a recursive artificial intelligence personality. Instead of the imaginary cosy den overflowing with brewskis, Bus resided on a small quantum chip nestled somewhere in this roving sarcophagus. It was the brain of a steel monster. Exactly where that chip was Douglas hadn't a clue, the location being a closely guarded trade secret of Volksoyota International. The thought made Douglas sad. It felt... lonely.

"Old Steelers fan?"

Douglas blinked. He was very confused, thinking that maybe it had come from the ad-play.

"Hey! Don't I know you?"

Douglas turned to square 87, barely believing what had just happened. A smaller man, bald on the top with a wildly hirsute, grey beard like a briar patch looked up at him through coke bottle glasses. A flashing, dancing 'living ink' tattoo of a mascot for a beverage company he had never heard of danced merrily across the man's arm. His mouth was upturned in the tightest smile Douglas had ever seen. He smelled heavily of a nostalgic smokey scent that was just foreign enough to drive Douglas mad trying to think of what it was. He frowned. Normally Douglas would ignore anyone talking to him remotely near the vicinity of Bus let alone while riding it. That wasn't his rule, by the way, it is just something that one does not do on modern public transit. In this instance however it would prove to be a fortuitous faux pas on his part.

"I don't believe so..." he answered before willing himself to shut up.

It was too late.

The social dance had begun.

Douglas began to sweat.

"No, no," the man ran his hand through his beard thoughtfully, little white flakes drifting down like a gentle snow, "I'm positive I know you from somewhere."

"Mmmhmm," replied Douglas, turning his attention back to the monitor suspended above the row in front of him. If he focused on the TV intently, maybe the man would desist in forcing this conversation. A commercial for cereal was playing, a cartoon frog hocking forty essential vitamins and nutrients. A gaggle of screaming children seemed zealously keen to eat the said cereal, a slow motion shot of synthetic vitamilk flooding like a New Brunswick tide against the multi-coloured flake shores of cereal island. Douglas couldn't make out the fine print scrolling along the bottom of the screen, even when he squinted. The few words he could make out were chance, diarrhea, condition, heart, consult, doctor and discontinue.

“Do you live in the Grand?”

Douglas gritted his teeth. Why wasn’t this man leaving him alone? Didn’t he know the bus was no place for small talk?

“The Grand? The arco-tenement on the river?”

“Arcology. But yes; duh.”

Douglas shook his head. The thought of living in the towering filth and crime infested arcology made him feel queasy. The monitor had changed from the cereal advertisement. Blue and white light flashed through out the bus as the hyper fast images of hockey players laying vicious bodychecks against each other played to some classic Metallica music. Some old player turned analyst screamed at them, expressing just how important the game between the Ontario Palm Leafs and the visiting Green Bay Hurricanes was to the ongoing happiness and continued success of society. The sports package was too expensive for Douglas to afford, so he would just have to try and carry on without watching.

“Allentown?”

Douglas snapped his attention back to the diminutive man. “I beg your pardon?”

“Allentown Arco?”

Douglas shook his head. “No.”

"Tonawanda Tower? Peche? Rose City Heights?"

"No, no, no," he replied, waving his hand dismissively, "I live up near Old Kitts."

"Old Kitts?" The man's face screwed up as he digested Douglas' answer. "That's not an arco. Or I don't know that arco, which is hard to believe. I know everything about arcos."

Shaking his head Douglas corrected him. "That would be because it's not an arco. It's one of the old cities."

"Old Kitts," the man repeated, "Never heard of it."

"That wasn't its actual name, I think. Saint something or other."

"Oh."

"Yes, it was a long time ago."

"Ahhhh. Pre-war?" he asked.

"Pre-pre-war," corrected Douglas.

"Ah. I wouldn't know anything about that," he said, scratching his cheek with immaculate fingernails, "I came up here in '65 with the Creole wave out of the old state of Louisiana. Most of the old GLAT had been blasted into kingdom-come and still rebuilding by then. Came to work on the Arcos, you know." The small man was pensive for a moment, before shrugging dismissively. "Gross."

A flash of annoyance roiled across Douglas before he could consciously suppress it. “Gross?” He asked.

To the diminutive man’s credit, his face bloomed rouge in embarrassment. “Sorry, sorry. Didn’t mean to be a dick. It’s just, you know…”

Douglas did not reply, hoping his silence and intensive concentration on the ad-play currently blaring out of the tv sets could discourage him from this unseemliness. This ad-play was for toilet paper, from his good friends at Proctor & Lockheed Martinez. Douglas made a mental note to pick some up before he went home.

“You look pretty normal.”

His heart jumping into his throat, Douglas turned bewilderingly to his right. A slight woman of advanced years, curly grey hairs bursting from the edges of a tightly secured Tilly hat, she was petite in comparison to the lanky Douglas.

“Excuse me?” He asked her.

“You look normal. For a no-hab. You said you’re a no-hab, aren’t you?”

Douglas could barely comprehend what was happening, now that two total strangers were talking to him. He could barely countenance his poor luck, being bussed between two chatty Cathy’s. Didn’t they know it was widely considered to be exceptionally rude to talk to anyone at anytime on the bus? Douglas was positive it was an unwritten rule somewhere. He tried to calculate the odds of such misfortune but found it difficult to concentrate as his two fellow passengers began to crosstalk, Douglas utterly aghast as he was caught in their crossfire of words.

"Oh, he's definitely a no-hab," decreed the man. Douglas nearly swooned as the man reached through his personal space, offering an outstretched hand to the woman. Douglas cringed as he nearly touched him. "Fred. Pleasure to meet you!"

The lady smiled and accepted the proffered greeting. "A pleasure! I'm Verna."

"Well Verna, my new friend here..." both looked at him with polite expectation.

It took Douglas half a heartbeat to realize 'new friend' was him, and that he was being prompted for his name. "Oh! Ah, I am Douglas." Douglas felt dirty.

"Pleasure to meet you, Doug," said the woman, barely above a whisper, while patting his arm. "I don't believe I've seen a no-hab in at least a decade."

"Is that so," murmured Doug politely but neutrally. He turned his attention to the video screen again, beginning to get annoyed by all the ad-plays he was missing. Douglas enjoyed his time on bus watching sponsored truths from various companies.

"Is that so," she continued, oblivious to Douglas' tone. "There can't be more than a hundred no-habs left on the whole peninsula."

"Maybe even less," chimed in Fred, leaning uncomfortably close into Douglas' spot, "Last incentive for relocation was... what? Five, ten years ago? My arco- Allentown- jumped another twenty thousand people in the first month alone! Can you imagine that? Twenty thousand new habs."

The old woman let out a low whistle at the number. The thought alone of just *that* many people all sharing the same living space made Douglas' stomach do somersaults. And those numbers were just a drop in the ocean.

"And that was just the first month," continued Fred excitingly, "The rest of the year saw three times as many abandon their homes for the easy living of Arco life! Can you imagine the logistical headache of relocating that many people from around the Great Lakes into a single Arcology?"

Fred let the silence between them grow until he realized no one was going to answer his rhetorical question.

"Quite the headache I tell you!"

"I believe it," said Verna, "I can remember when I moved into Peche Trees. Our intake group was the full five hundred thousand. It was quite the adventure!" She laughed, but the trill of her mirth was tinged with a memory of anxiousness that Douglas could not help but notice. She continued. "That was... oh, thirty years ago or so-"

"Then you were one of the first intakes!" Fred exclaimed.

Verna nodded. "That's right." Douglas watched as her mind fell inward, travelling through time to a world long dead. The wrinkles on her face looked older, more tired, as her memory took her back. She could still imagine the screams of the old Canucks that were refusing to leave their homes, some of them on land their family had cultivated for centuries. That counted for little when weighed against the muzzle of a gun, however, so in the end their resistance counted for less than little. Verna collected herself and flashed a smile at Fred across an increasingly perturbed Douglas. "How did you know that? That I was one of the first?"

Douglas was afraid that the satisfied grin on Fred's face might break with how happy he seemed. Reaching into his coat, he made a slow and dramatic show of pulling forth a plastic card attached to a rainbow lanyard dangling around his neck. The card was very simple in design- a small black and white BQR code below the logo of residential arcology construction and operating firm Allied Advanced Arcologies.

“I was there!” He proclaimed proudly, laughing loudly enough that most of the bus turned to see what the hell was going on. Douglas was ashamed enough at the boisterous behaviour to cringe for all of them. Verna laughed along politely at a much quieter decibel level. The TV was playing a commercial for moonside industries, propaganda on behalf of the Lunar Business Association resplendent with an ethnically diverse cast of happy-looking actors pretending to gleefully mine ice and swinging around on lunar gravity golf courses. It did not entice Douglas in the slightest.

“Yup,” continued Fred, at no one’s bequest, “I’ve been an arco-man my entire life! Right out of university I joined up.”

Douglas really could not find a way to care less. Verna seemed at least somewhat interested.

“Is that so?” She asked, “What do you do for them?”

“What haven’t I done you mean,” he laughed, “I’ve worked on every arco in the GLAT. Sanitation, agriculture, internment, security, repossession, compost – that sucked the most. I could list them all but suffice to say not many people know the big buildings the way I do!" He beamed at them expectantly, and after an awkward pause Douglas found his voice.

"Oh. Wow." He smiled tepidly.

"That is very impressive, Fred," said Verna in a kindly, patronizing voice.

Fred took no heed of the tone. "You're right- it is! Thank you, Verna," he smiled back, "I bet you'll never guess what I do now!"

Douglas found that he could, indeed, care less.

"Hmmm," said Verna, happy to indulge the man. Douglas returned his gaze to the TV- he reverted to his strategy that if he stared at it intently enough, he could pretend he was being left alone. The current program was another adplay- in this one, a sponsored truth on behalf of the Asian Zone Consortium proudly claimed with an ethnically uniform cast of happy-looking actors pretending to gleefully mine lithium and singing in a thousand strong chorus the merits of working in Asia under the fatherly gaze of the Grand Patriotic Union. Without a doubt every single one of those actors was an AI simulacrum; normal human actors mostly stuck to live theatre. The adplay didn't entice Douglas in the slightest.

"Maybe," Verna began, a slight smile as she considered the small and loud man. Douglas' held in a gasp as the horror that she was enjoying this social interaction dawned on him. "Are you a RO?" she finally guessed.

Fred smiled again. "A residence overseer? I *have* been one, once upon a time. But not anymore! Nope, now I am in fact-"

The blue lights promptly switched to an alarming red as Bus' face promptly appeared on the monitors. Fred looked alarmed, while Douglas looked like he had bit a lemon, upset that the renovation show Master Arcobuster Hab Brothers had been just about to come on. Instead, Bus was on all the monitors. Gone was the amiable and genial face of the moustachioed AI. In its place was a countenance that bore the dread promise of emotionless order, a computer-generated djinn floating above them, with a paternalistic sneer that conveyed perfectly how disappointed Bus was.

"I apologize to our guests- UGLTA endeavours to make every ride safe and sound for each and every one of our valued customers. I must make sure that the safety of our riders is paramount- to this effect, any type of violence is inexcusable on any UGTLA conveyance. If you do not refrain from your current behaviour, I will be forced to neutralize you."

Douglas looked around in alarm, only calming down by the fact that Bus did not seem to be referring to anyone on their level. Bus hovered there, a dozen heads repeated on a dozen monitors basking in the red glow of the pulsing lights, the steady rhythm of Bus breathing, his mechanical heart beating in unified timing. Everyone else on the bus held their breath. The face of their digital pilot was a mask of frozen authority, waiting patiently for whoever was causing problems to return to the docile state expected of the modern public transit traveller.

The bus hummed and bounced, moving along the highway at its usual breakneck pace. The bus was as silent as a tomb but for the siren and strobing red light. At least from what Douglas could see and hear. He hoped that whoever was causing trouble was settling down.

"This is your last warning."

Bus' voice was unlike in tenor than his usual affable self. That did not bode well. Gone was the happy and welcoming face of the Transit Authority. Now a dark presence permeated Bus. Douglas' ears strained as a muffled cry was interrupted by a staccato rumbling from somewhere below. A few people cried out in alarm as the bus shook with recoil. Douglas' stomach roiled as the vehicle came to such a sudden stop that the inertial dampeners could not counter-affect the lurching forward motion. Someone on their level retched audibly as vertigo washed over the passengers like in a wave pool.

With a pleasant accompanying ding, the lights changed back to blue. It mollified Douglas a little.

Bus' smiling face had returned.

"Ah jeez, oh boy, I am sooooo," Bus dragged the word out for at least three seconds, "sorry, folks, I'm afraid we're going to have to evacuate you all from the bus due to an unplanned maintenance event. We'll be doing this nice and orderly, ok? Please step forward as your section is lit. No pushing, folks!"

A loud groan escaped every passenger's lips except for Fred's. Douglas shook his head, not believing his terrible luck. A disembark would put him way behind schedule, uncountably so if the rain fell on them while they waited. He could picture his partner's face when he would have to tell her he missed his appointment and that the UBI wasn't coming this month. Douglas breath began to sharpen and increase in frequency as his mouth went dry.

"Well, what the hell is this?" Asked Fred sourly.

Verna shook her head. "Pretty common, is what it is. Too Jobs damn common."

Fred looked confused. "Common?"

Douglas opened his mouth before he even knew he was responding. If he had managed to catch himself, he most certainly would have rode the wait out silently. "Yes, it is fairly common. Unfortunately. Now we'll have to disembark."

Fred looked around wildly. "Disembark? Whatever for?"

Verna gave him a queer look. "Well, yes; they'll need to clean up wherever the... maintenance happened."

Douglas intuited what was happening. "Fred... is this your first time riding Bus?"

Fred snapped his attention around to Douglas. "How in the devil did you know that?"

Douglas scuffed his foot against the ground sheepishly as he looked Fred in the eyes. "Well, you don't know what a disembark is. That's a pretty big clue that you're new to riding Bus."

Fred shook his head. "So... what is a disembark?"

Douglas looked down at Verna, who had completely withdrawn into herself.

Douglas floundered for words. “It’s, ah, well. We all need to get off the bus.”

Fred nodded dumbly, not quite sure what was going on.

It was a good thirty minutes of the most excruciating small talk Douglas had ever been subjected to until the lights on their level turned a bright white, banishing all shadows from Bus and revealing the interior for what it was. Thick black stains like zebra stripes covered the ground, creating an argyle pattern with the yellow paint, while stripped loose wires and sad dented panels hung in sad clumps in various places around the ceiling. A pile of what most likely was human excrement was far too close to Douglas’ foot than he was comfortable with. The passengers, starting at the front, began to file out of the bus in slow single file. The elevator to the exit acted like a choke point, adding at least a good minute delay in extricating each passenger as they reached the front. After what seemed like an eternity, Douglas shuffled to the sliding door and entered the tight confines of the people mover. At first everything proceeded according to plan, the way it had a hundred times before, the trite muzak playing joyfully.

No virtual landscape this time, which should have been his first clue something was amiss. The second clue was the red drip marks slowly drying along the floor.

As the elevator reached the bottom, Douglas' horror grew as a red frothy liquid poured onto the floor, seeping in through any and all available cracks in the elevator.

He tried to position his feet so that they remained apart from the tide of bubbly fluid and soap seeping into the elevator. This proved to be futile, as the whining surge of pressure washers cleansing the main floor reached the front of the bus, expelling a soupy mass of viscera into the elevator. Douglas looked skywards, intently ignoring the crimson tide of blood rushing in around his ankles.

Chapter Three New Fam Ride Dat Bondo

Just as he thought he could take no more, the front doors split open, and Douglas gasped as he propelled himself forward, a disheveled fetus with red-stained pant cuffs birthed from the hole of a gargantuan beast of steel skin and silicon brains. The thick mixture of blood, water, soap and all one of a dozen mystery liquids cascaded from Bus' open mouth down onto the black tarmac beneath his feet. Douglas quickly stepped forward into the bewildered mass of people blinking in the scorching midday sun, many reaching into pockets and purses for shaded glasses. The heat at this hour was already unbearable- the trauma teams from the GLAT hospital-arcos had already arrived on scene, and pop-up tents had been erected to protect the bus passengers from the dangers of the relentless inferno that was 10:00 AM in the Great Lakes.

“Holy shit!” Said Fred as he stumbled out of the bus, using Douglas as an unwilling steadying post as he tried to regain his composure. “What the hell is that!?” He exclaimed, pointing down at the diluted mess pooling around the front Bus’ doors. Bus’ face was on the panel next to the door, smiling at an irate woman demanding recompense for the interrupted ride.

“Aw well jeez, oh boy,” said Bus, nodding his head as she continued to berate him, “Oh yes, yes, I see why me killing him would make you upset. Oh yes. Yes. Yes. Is that so? Well I sure am sorry Lynn, but by agreeing to ride with any Great Lakes Transit Authority conveyance, and of being allowed to participate in a Bus ride, you agreed to release and discharge UGLTA officers, employees, volunteers, holograms, androids, artificial intelligent, and UGLTA agents from any and all claims, liabilities, demands, actions, or causes of action arising out of your participation or other passengers participation inside me! So, you sure are out of luck. What was that? No, Lynn, that is physically impossible to do to myself, as I am just Bus and not anatomically equipped for such things."

Douglas squinted as he gazed at their surroundings. The sun was a quarter of the way in the sky, and the way it reflected off any somewhat glossy surface made it terribly blinding. They had stopped near the Patriots Skyway on the southern shore of what once was great lake Ontario, a long and high concrete suspension bridge spanning the Hamilton dustbowl. Thick clouds of black smoke rose from across the old bay in Hamilton proper, flames licking at their undersides wantonly from the smokestacks and forges running continuously to produce the steel needed to maintain and expand the GLAT. Flaming rivers of slag spilled from giant's iron cups at the lip of the old shore, tumbling down nearly twenty meters into the hardpacked clay of the old lakebed. Where the slag came to rest the land steamed, what little water there was this time of year hiding in the clay evaporating instantly in plumes of angry white vapour.

"Well, this sucks," said Fred, walking up alongside Douglas and slapping him on the back. A reflective pair of wrap-around shades covered half the man's head, accompanied by a popular style of wide-brim hat the kids called umbies. It made the man's head look small. Fred pointed down at his shoes and tsk-tsked.

"I guess you don't mess with Bus, eh? My pants are ruined! Look at my shoes. Steven Jobs on a stick! Fuck whoever that guy was! And you say this is normal? Jobs be good." Douglas was not a fan of such familiar contact or liberal potty-mouthery, but maintained a stiff upper lip and took it in stride. "Look at this absolute shithole. No wonder Bus has no windows, eh?"

Douglas nodded politely.

The overly-familiar man was not wrong, Douglas agreed silently. Ruin and rubble surrounded them in equal measure. The road curved back behind them until they lost sight of it behind a small, crumbled apartment building. It looked like the building had been sheared off at the thirty-first floor, with the upper twenty or so sliding down and coming to rest in a mangled pile of steel and concrete across half the old highway. No one had ever bothered to clean it up, and there was not a zero chance that the pile was highly radioactive. To their north lay the old shore of what was once Lake Ontario. Blasted out wreckages of battle-vehicles still lay where they fell, the ground around them too laden with explosive mines as to warrant the risk of recovery.

They were still half an hour bus ride from the outskirts of Downtown proper, or roughly a sixteen hour walk. Even a half an hour walk outside in the heat of the day would undoubtedly kill most of them.

"So…" Fred rocked back on his heels, "What happens now?"

"They'll send another bus to pick us up." Verna, in the daylight, did not seem so old as Douglas had thought back in the dimness of the bus. She held a parasol over her shoulder, looking quite comfortable despite the ferocious heat. Her pants were still immaculate, and her shoes fresh as if they had just come off an assembly line. "They'll make us use our free ride to board. It'll probably be a couple of hours."

Douglas nodded in agreement. Fred was still focused on Verna.

"How did you not get soaked?" asked Fred, clearly jealous.

"Not my first 'customer service incident' on Bus," she answered with a wink, to which Fred laughed. "I took off my shoes before getting in the lift."

"Jesus, is that what they actually call it?" Fred looked skeptical. Douglas looked bored.

"A CSI? Believe it or not, they do," nodded Verna.

Douglas nodded in agreement.

“So,” said Fred slowly, “Bus will just up and 401 a guy if he’s a nuisance? Crazy. You’ve seen this before, too, Dougy?”

Douglas nodded in agreement, despite being called Dougy.

“Then why on Earth didn’t you take your shoes off?”

Douglas shrugged.

“You’re a weird guy, Doug,” said Fred shaking his head, “A couple hour wait? In this heat? Ha! Yah I don’t think so.”

Fred reached into his pocket and pulled out his phone. Walking a few steps away, he began barking orders into the phone in a language Douglas didn’t recognize.

“What an odd fellow,” remarked Verna, stepping up beside Douglas. “Seriously; who talks to people on Bus?”

“Yes!” Douglas exclaimed, maybe a little too vehemently. “I honestly couldn’t believe what he was doing!”

“Same, same,” agreed Verna, “I have to admit, I kind of enjoyed it.”

Douglas shrugged and nodded silently, not wanting to disagree with the kind old lady.

Fred walked back towards them, grinning widely. "So! You'll never guessed what I do for a living now!"

Douglas was in no mood for games. He shook his head but didn't say anything.

Verna shook her head as well.

"Ah, you folks are no fun. Well, let's just say the word executive is in my company title. And with that title comes certain perks. Here comes one of the perks now."

After a few minutes an unholy sound screamed in from the west. It sounded like a mix between a diesel engine and a rutting bull. After a minute the sleek profile of a gryphon came soaring into view from behind the Skyway. The sunlight reflected off the windshield and the glossy black panels emblazoned with the AAA logo. It's wings fluttered in the wind as the bio-organism glided down in a tightening gyre, like in some great unseen whirlpool. It let out an ear-piercing shriek from its beak, while the bonded mechanical apparatus let out a merry honk of its horn.

"Holy shit, is that a bondo?" Exclaimed a younger man excitedly.

The Bondo- slang for bonded organism- was a luxury vehicle from the life-loving bio-engineers at Metatastic Prime, a conglomerate of early internet companies that pivoted hard to genetic modification research at the birth of the second internet. Bioengineering, according to the history books, had been very much resisted by large segments of society. This was largely due to the fact that animals crossed with machines are, to use one contemporary politician's words, ‘Gross as hell’. They nearly went bankrupt until the unveiling of the aerial predator transport, aptly called the gryphon. A semi-intelligent cyborg that could out-speed a jet in a precision dive, out-fight a hippopotamus with its landing gear, heal itself, repair itself (to a degree) all while carrying a platoon of heavily armed soldiers. Within a year MP had become the largest private defense contractor in the world. This current model was light years ahead of the first one, a private civilian transport model that could still rip through a company of soldiers if it cared to.

“Not bad, eh?” Asked Fred, grinning wildly. The gryphon came to a landing a few metres in front of them, it’s large talons breaking into the asphalt like hungry teeth into an apple. Douglas shook his head in disapproval. Taxpayer money would have to repair that. His money. Not that a company man like Fred gave a damn. People with employment rarely thought about the cost of things.

“Holy crap Paps,” effused the young man, having walked up beside them. He was shorter than Douglas, with green hair in a tight bun on top of his head, the rest being shorn clean to scalp. His shades were public school issue Soblaws brand cheap plastic, the made in Newfoundland seal of crappiness proudly stamped on the side. He wore no coat over his freckled, sun-burned skin, and his shirt was an old faded hand me down, a tour shirt advertising the early classical rock band Pearl Jam. Douglas didn’t much care for music, and would be hard-pressed at gunpoint to name a single popular, contemporary song. It all sounded just like noise to him. The young man laughed gleefully. “Ma fam ain’t ever gonna believe dis, ken it?”

“Oh, I ken,” Fred answered, his voice taking on a north-arco accent. “Ya be noobin’ on dat bondo, fam?”

The young man laughed along with Fred. Even Verna joined in. Douglas smiled politely, his cheeks hurting with the strain of forcing it all.

“Yes, yes sir,” replied the young man when the laughter subsided. His patois, a mix of old English and various southern countries, was a slang developed in the densest of the arcos in the northern territories. “I’ve seen them on the ‘net, obvs. Zero in real life. Your norco slang is spot on, sir! You habbin’ up in Toronto?”

“Why thank you, young man,” replied Fred graciously, “I don’t live in Toronto, no, but I did help build it!”

The young man’s eyes went even wider. “No way!” He exclaimed.

“Been an AAA man all my life!”

“That’s chingy, sir!” Douglas hadn’t the slightest clue what they were going on about, but he did pick out the word Toronto.

“Toronto? Are you heading to Toronto, Fred?” He asked hopefully.

“Nope!” Replied Fred cheerfully, “But I will be happy to give my new friends a ride! I can drop you off there on my way.”

Verna let out a happy cry and clapped her hands. The young man began to jump around in excitement. He introduced himself as Trite, a content producer for a social influencer, which is to say self-employed, which was to say unemployed, and began to profusely thank Fred who merely laughed it off graciously.

A sense of relief washed over Douglas for the first time in months. He wasn’t going to miss his PO appointment after all. His previous waking nightmare turned into one of a happy partner, smiling and pleased with him. Douglas thought about how today was full of surprises. He surprised himself with one more as they walked towards the gryphon.

“Thank you, Fred,” he told his new friend. And he meant it. “I have got to ask you- if this was an option, why on Earth were you riding Bus?”

Fred laughed, easily and warmly.

“Honestly? I woke up this morning, and I just had the idea. So, I went for it!”

Douglas gave Fred a reappraising look. “You just... went for it?”

Fred nodded. “Yup.”

“Oh,” said Fred, unsure of how to respond. ‘Going for it’ was a phrase not in his vocabulary.

“I would hazard a guess that you’re not the type to make spontaneous decisions. Is that fair?”

Douglas nodded sheepishly.

Fred clutched his arm and spoke earnestly as they walked. “Doug, you absolutely must. Life is terrible enough- it will pass you right by if you let it! Grab the bull by the horns! Don’t look and take the jump. It’s what keeps one young.”

Douglas considered that as they boarded the gryphon, taking their seats in the six-seater general cabin. Douglas sunk gladly into the lush beige leather seat across from Fred near the cockpit entrance, while

Verna and Trite took the two seats in the middle. Douglas suppressed a delighted moan as he got comfortable, while Fred kicked off his shoes and laughed at the wide smile growing across his face.

“Now this is luxury,” purred Trite, stretching out in his seat.

“You best believe it, son,” promised Fred, “Triple-A looks after it’s people, I’ll tell you that much.”

Douglas had to admit Fred wasn’t wrong. The cabin was luxuriously spacious and generously stocked with amenities, even for a company bondo. Douglas knew that this stranger-now-turned-friend had been a company man his whole life, but now he was beginning to get really curious about Fred. There was a soft thick carpet across the whole floor, individual monitors for each seat, haptic VR ports in the chairs, a large bar along the back wall stocked with drinks and snacks. Most corporate suits Douglas knew, which was personally zero, were paid peanuts, or straight up for reductions in indentured credit. Even worse were those who worked solely for company scrip, people that Douglas thought of as being no more than literal slaves. God knows Douglas had never made the kind of money or had the kind of position that resulted in these kinds of perks. Whoever

Fred was, he was undeniably high up in the world of Arco construction.

The curtain at the front of the cabin parted and the pilot walked into the cabin. He was a thick man of middle years, a large brown beard braided down his chest and a crescent moon tattooed on his cheek. A flight cap perched precariously atop his head, seemingly one size too small. He laughed as he walked into the back.

"What did I tell you, Fred?" He chortled, carrying on in a thick and loud Scandinavian accent. "I told you it was a bad idea, did I not? A bloody pack of savages they are-"

The pilot cut short as he eyed the three additional passengers. He coughed into the crook of his elbow. "Ah, I see we have guests," he said, trying to retain a modicum of professionalism, "I am, ah, sorry for what I said."

None of them accepted the apology, as none of them warranted he had anything to apologize about. It is exceedingly difficult to maintain the moral high ground after wading through the remnants of a person murdered by a sentient automobile. The three men's stained pant cuffs gave credence to the appellation of savage.

“Nonsense, Dunkan. You were right- it was positively dreadful. Stinky and dark and surprisingly violent. Completely terrible experience. Except for the company!”

Fred introduced each of them to Victor in turn, no different than how someone would introduce a long-missed friend. It warmed Douglas’ heart slightly, and his thoughts turned to the Moodmen. Surely it wouldn’t hurt to just have a look, especially now that his bus fare had been refunded and the unplanned customer service debarkation had given him the boon of the free ride home. Douglas nodded, whispering to himself. “Got to take the jump.”

“So, where we all headed?” Duncan smiled at the passengers. Fred took charge effortlessly. “We will be stopping off at Toronto my good man to drop off these fine fellows. Then we can carry on to the Castle.”

“Castle?” Douglas asked.

“Yes, a castle! Never mind that though- you’re going to miss a helluva view!”

The gryphon bounded along the highway for a good 10 metres before coiling up its hind legs and bounding up into the air. It didn’t come back down. Outside the window to Douglas’s left a large eagle wing, the size of a grand piano, spread out before him, the feathers rippling in the wind, as if someone was playing the tips like piano keys.

The wings began to beat furiously but silently beyond the double plastiglass shield of the window. The wings were so close that Douglas could have touched it if not for the barrier. He could see the muscles in the wing working with such force that it was terrifying to a man as cognizant of his mortality as Douglas. The hundreds of people left behind on the ground looked up in a mix of awe, disgust, and jealousy. That is until being buffeted back as the auxiliary engines on it's hindquarters fired up. The ones who managed to maintain their footing stared up at them with their hands shielding the sun glare, while the others went scattering like leaves on the wind. As they ascended into heaven away from the savages below Douglas found it was fun to pretend, if just for this moment, that he was not one of them.

The gryphon banked hard to the west flying over the sands of the old Hamilton Harbour until it could spread its wings, lifting itself on the draft of air coming from the never-ending waterfall of slag heating the sands below into molten glass. The excavator AI's tasked with moving the cooled slag down below turned their sensors up to track the bondo passing overhead. From this height Douglas pretended they were children's toys.

The gryphon snapped its wings outwards, catching the up draft, lifting them, higher, higher, higher into the sky. Having never been this high up before in his life (this did not include the inside of an arcology- those views were a great deal less impressive) Douglas was amazed as the land shrunk below him, as if a great map was being unrolled before him. His breath caught in his throat at the stunning vista only airflight can provide, and he could feel his eyes moisten at the beauty of it.

The entirety of the Niagara peninsula was laid out before him. On the far horizon he could make out the rising steams from Niagara Falls, that once great wonder of the world now a pale wraith of its former majesty. Banks of transformers, batteries, and electrical towers kilometres high criss-crossed across the landscape, the bones of a great beast that had devoured a once greener land. Infinite kilometres of wire and cable snaked like veins across the skin of the land. They combined into greater and greater strands as they spread towards their beating heart at the Adam Beck power generating station. Bundles of cables, dozens of yards thick, shined in the light of the sun. Douglas thought they were oily indigo aortas, leading back to a black and bloated heart thrumming with coruscant energies.

Nearer to them, Douglas could see the cables give way to at first small dwellings, the like of which he resided in. He was pretty sure he could see his house from up here but was in fact looking in the entirely wrong place. The thought made him happy though. The further east he looked, the bigger the buildings began to grow. They ringed the old harbour and the forges in a tight embrace. Packed together, one on top of each other, some rose higher than its siblings around it, while others had collapsed and were now leaning into its neighbours. It was a vast haphazard skeleton of a city, a necropolis void of life. At least on the surface; appearances were often deceiving nowadays.

Every single one of them- each single one of untold thousands- were empty and abandoned by any sane citizen living in the Greater Lakes Arcology Territory. The scars of urbanization from a long-ago age still remained all these decades later. No one with their wits went there anymore, the government and corporations having written off most of it before Douglas was even born. Criminals and mutants lived there now, or so he was told. Or maybe it was just degenerates or perhaps just the unlucky. Douglas empathized with them a bit, feeling that they might just share some things in common.

"Isn't it something?" asked Fred breathlessly, standing up and walking over to Douglas. He leaned against the window and pointed towards the graveyard of towering tombstones. "To imagine all of this was once inhabited. It's almost unbelievable, eh?"

Douglas did not stand, his body completely unwilling to extricate itself from the throes of comfort. He eyed the same buildings dubiously. "Is that so? All of them?"

Fred nodded. "After the temp went up and the tropics and southern states turned into a scorched-out hell, the GLAT become one of the most densely populated places on Earth. The old nations couldn't manage the sudden influx of hundreds of millions. When the food riots started the toll of destruction was damn near unimaginable. Neighbour against neighbour. I remember as a child watching a women get stabbed for a loaf of bread. Do you remember those times, Douglas? Before the Arcos?"

Douglas nodded tersely. He tried not to think of those days. "I'm afraid my childhood was a fairly unhappy one, and best left in the past."

Fred looked alarmed, holding up his hands palms outwards. “Oh, Jobs damn it. I’m sorry Douglas, I didn’t mean to upset you.”

Douglas did not look in the slightest way upset. “That’s ok, Fred. I’m fine. I’m just the type of guy who thinks more about the future.” His thoughts turned to his partner, and he wondered what they were up to.

“Ever think of going to the Moodmen?”

The question startled Douglas. Turning in his seat, he faced Verna.

“Pardon me, Verna?” Asked Douglas. Fred returned to his seat, a pensive look on his face.

“Have you ever gone to the Moodmen?” She repeated.

“No,” began Douglas slowly, “I was actually thinking of going today.”

“Oh, you absolutely must,” she gushed, “It has done absolute wonders for my phobias.”

“Is that so,” said Fred, and something in the tone of his voice made Douglas curious as to what the eccentric man was thinking.

“It’s true, Fred. I was deathly afraid of spiders- now I’m proud to say my house is a catch and release home!”

Trite made a retching sound that Douglas found rude but elicited a laugh from Fred. “Catch and release!?

No heat ma'am, but if one of them pack of coyote spiders comes after me I'm gonna," he mimed spraying the cabin with an imaginary rifle, "blat blat blat!"

Verna scoffed at the young man. "I didn't mean the big ones! The little ones that haven't been mutated."

"Mutated?" Asked Trite.

"Mutated," added Fred shaking his head, "What on Earth do they teach in school nowadays. Spiders used to be no bigger than a hand- most no bigger than a fingernail! Radiation has mutated them into the dog-like creatures we have today."

"Get out of town," said Trite, clearly not believing them.

"It's true," insisted Verna, "The small corpse and dock spiders around here are the ones I release. I think their webs are just beautiful in the morning light."

Douglas nodded. He thought so as well.

"The Peche trees arco," said Fred out of nowhere. He stared out the window to the south. "There it is right there- the one with the circular top."

Douglas turned to look. On the horizon, well past the highways of electrical cable, the towering monstrosity that was the 320 stories tall Peche Trees arcology stood proud against the morning light. The top was shaped roughly like a peach- Douglas had heard that long ago some of the best peaches in the world had come from the area where he now lived. Douglas had never tasted a peach in his life; only peach-flavoured synth-fruit. This peach was wholly inedible, and even if by some fantastical chance it was, no mouth was big enough to take a reasonable bite out of it.

“What deets, fam?” Asked Trite.

“I was there when we broke ground on it. There was a family of wolf-spiders living in an underground hive- somehow the geodesic AI fouled up the survey and misinterpreted the data. The AI of course blamed it on human error. In any case- it was about an hour in when the excavator broke into the hive. The excavation team never got a chance to blame anyone.”

Fred went quiet for a moment, clearly visiting somewhere else, sometime else in his mind. The faint hum of the bondo’s engine was the only sound. Perhaps it was only the rustle of time on the wind.

“Then what happened?” Asked Douglas quietly.

Fred looked at Douglas in surprise, then at Verna and Trite quickly before smiling. “Sorry, my friend? What were we talking about?”

“Peche Trees,” breathed Trite.

“The spiders,” added Verna.

“Oh, yes, of course, silly me,” laughed Fred, and the rest of them laughed as well, each for a different reason; one for pity, one for empathy and one for genuine mirth.

“Well, it took the better part of a week to completely clear the hive. The bereavement costs alone nearly bankrupted us. Could you imagine? If AAA had gone under?”

“I’m sure someone else would have picked up the torch,” assured Verna.

“Don’t be so sure, madame,” replied Fred knowingly, waving a finger.

Whatever Fred said next was lost in the blaring of the alarm, a deafening eagle’s cry from the mouth of the Bondo. Dunkan’s voice cut in over the alarm, his thick accent almost indecipherable. “Buckle-up buckaroo’s! We have incoming!”

Fred quickly stumbled back to his chair, falling into it face first as the floor beneath him tilted beneath him. He barely managed to grab hold of the restraining belt, using it as a lifeline to pull himself into the seat. Douglas let out a sharp exhale of relief as Fred in a mad scramble got his seatbelt on as the cabin jostled and rolled around them.

Trite let out an exuberant cheer as the floor fell out from underneath them. Douglas lifted a few inches up off his chair as they went into freefall, the Bondo tucking its wings close to its body. As they sped faster in the tight dive, looking out the window Douglas could see fresh contrails, white snakes speeding towards them through the air.

Following the contrails back, Douglas could see that they came from the mass of empty buildings across the old harbor. His knuckles went white as he gripped the armrest of the seat, desperate to hang on to not only the chair, but also his lunch.

The Gryphon rolled in the air. The restraints bit into the passengers as their weightless free-fall bodies were twisted and turned, at the mercy of the bondos movements. The pilot and the gryphon operated as one in their desperate attempt to escape the surface to air missiles closing in on them.

“Releasing chaff,” warned Duncan over the loudspeaker. A moment later, the gryphon shook with violent force as a deafening explosion, then another and another detonated behind them. The bondo shook violently. Verna let out a shriek. Douglas began to think that the vibrations would literally shake the bondo apart.

“Leveling out!” yelled Duncan. The warning meant little and less to Douglas, this being the first time he had flown, or been subject to rocket fire, or been shot at while flying. Today was beginning to become a day of firsts.

Having already forgotten the warning in the face of existential terror and fragile mortality, Douglas accidentally bit his tongue as the gryphon sharply exited its dive. The wings spread out again, and they sailed across the basin of the old harbour at breakneck speed, no more than a dozen metres above the old lakebed.

Douglas craned his neck to see how Verna and Trite were faring. Verna’s eyes were shut tight, her mouths working soundlessly in what might have been a prayer or merely a stream of curses. Trite seemed to be having the time of his life. A huge smile plastered across his face as he laughed wildly. Douglas wasn’t sure if the boy was mad or completely sane- what could one do but laugh in this situation? Other than quiet crying, which was Douglas’ usual choice of coping with stress.

Douglas thanked whatever company manufactured these seats for focusing so dearly on the cushions. As the bondo began to bob up and down on its level trajectory, the passengers bounced up just to be slammed down into their seats. A loud retching behind him and the smell of stomach bile filled the cabin. Looking back, Douglas saw Verna clutching an air waste bag, tears dripping from her eyes.

“We’re not out of the woods yet!” screamed Dunkan. The bondo screeched a new warning as two flashes of light from outside caught Douglas’s attention. From down in the sand not too far from the slag pit, two plumes of black smoke billowing out from two flaming missiles.

“Who the hell is firing at us from down there!?” yelled Douglas to no one in particular.

“It’s the damn AI,” yelled Fred, shaking his head angrily, “Their friend or foe recognition must be glitching! Fucking fofident AI bastard! Hold tight!”

Douglas was pretty sure they were all dead. It would be just his luck that his maiden flight would end with him exploded across the sand wastes.

With the most bone-shuddering crash Douglas had ever experienced, the bondo abruptly pounced down into the sand before springing up, twisting its arms towards the incoming missiles. A shower of sand, silicate and stone flung up and outwards from the gryphons taloned claws as it pivoted in the dirt. In one smooth swoop it was back up in the air, beatings its wings furiously as it sped away from the newly conjured screen of chaff.

The thudding booms of the two missiles exploding behind them was the sweetest sound Douglas had ever heard.

A tense minute of silence followed as the passengers held their breath, waiting for the next alarm. It never came.

“Well then,” said Fred finally, “Are we having fun?”

“Hell yah!” Yelled Trite, clapping wildly.

Douglas was less vocal about their thoughts on the ride so far.

“Well,” said Verna, “It still beats the Bus.”

Chapter Four
Arcology

The rest of the flight, at least after they had all calmed down from the excitement, was much quieter and less violent.

"Does that kind of thing happen often?" Verna asked Fred.

"Well," began Fred slowly, "It all depends on where you are I suppose. My usual flight takes off from the Niagara peninsula and takes a heading due north. There's a reason we don't fly this close to old Hamilton. A reason I imagine you three now understand better than most."

Douglas nodded.

"Well, the nice thing is it should be smooth sailing from here on out. Please, help yourselves to the mini-bar and enjoy the rest of the ride- I must make a phone call." He smiled, but Douglas could tell that it was forced as it never reached the corners of his mouth. Standing up, Fred disappeared through the front curtain to the forward cabin.

"This bondo is one tight mutie, ken it fam," expressed Trite as he sauntered over to the mini-bar, picking up a can of Coca-Cola. "Holy crap! This is legit Coca-Cola! Not New Coke!"

Douglas could not muster the same enthusiasm as the young man could for carbonated soft drinks. He did feel a modicum of excitement at the soft fruit sitting in a wire basket, only to have his hope come crashing down when it was obviously plastic to touch. Douglas wasn't all that surprised- actual fruit? That was a bridge too far to believe. Douglas hadn't eaten a banana in at least thirty years.

"Rain is still holding off," said Dunkan as the intercom crackled to life, "Helluva view as we come up on downtown!"

He wasn't wrong, Douglas thought.

The enormous city of Great Lakes Arcology Territory encompassed roughly two-thousand square kilometres of land, from the north at Georgian Bay to the great falls and warren of dry lake beds in the south.

The overwhelming majority of that was wasteland, what most rational people would consider uninhabitable but nonetheless was overflowing with those who Douglas would consider irrational, himself included. For those who wished to remain free from the towering monstrosities that were the arcologies, there weren't exactly a lot of options.

Downtown, what used to be called the Greater Toronto Area, was one of the most densely inhabited places on Earth. Home to no fewer than four dozen arcologies, Downtown at last census housed around 1 billion souls inside it's gigantic self-contained and self-sustained cities. The biggest of those, Toronto, housed 30 million people alone.

The sun peaked out from behind clouds beginning to roll in from the southeast, a mirror image of the ones rushing to meet them coming from the southwest. It was never good when two fronts met over the old lakebed.

Toronto loomed larger than all other arcologies, at least four dozen stories higher than the ones that had sprung up around its massive cylindrical tower shape. It was, if you can forgive the pun, a towering achievement of architecture. If it could be believed, the old city of Toronto was practically miniature compared to the sprawl of modern urban blight that was the warren of overground arcologies and underground tunnels. One could live in an arcology their entire life and never set foot outside- every arcology was its own self-contained city, completely able to survive with zero assistance from outside, if at least on a subsistence level. Hospitals, daycares, hydroponic farms, grocery, funeral services, AAVRs, placement offices, movie theatres, waterparks, prisons, universities'- all and more could be found in each and every arcology. Why step outside, why face the reality of the true world when you could live in comfort? It was not uncommon for children to have massive panic attacks when they stepped outside for the first time, completely unhinged by the lack of ceilings.

The summit of the Toronto arcology mushroomed out, numerous neon green landing platforms waiting with open arms for a variety of conventional and unconventional aerial transports. They looked to Douglas like ping-pong paddles laid out like branches on a massive tree trunk. Only a few arcologies boasted upper platforms for traffic- coincidentally, these were the same arcos populated by the most affluent of residents. A long and sinuous bondo, reminiscent of a Chinese dragon, coiled on one of the landing platforms decked in bright red and gold scales- undoubtedly a direct sub-orbital from Beijing. Hundreds of passengers piled out on the amber-coded platform, indicative of foreigners arriving in the USA. Vaguely humanoid AI-Drones lined the disembarkation ramps, steel claws stoically holding charge rifles, emotionless automatons with ever watchful eyes for the first sight of trouble.

The lower platforms were for inter-city transports- aircars and bondos servicing the elite from arco to arco. Douglas was tickled by the novelty of it all- he had only ever entered an arco from the ground level or lower. To see the arcos from this height was sobering- the ground far below was masked in fog and smog, an omnipresent blanket of pollution providing cover for some of the worst humanity had to offer. The upper part of the arcology shined blindingly, its countless windows acting like mirrors in the rising late morning sun.

"Coming up- Toronto. Please take your seats and buckle up. Should be a pretty easy landing all things considered."

Fred walked back into the cabin. His face was a mask of worry and consternation but only for a moment- the genial host from before returned almost instantly as he rejoined his passengers.

"Well, here we are, my friends," he said amiably, "Toronto as promised. I hope our little incident didn't turn you off from traveling Air Bondo! Ha!"

The gryphon came soaring in after circling the arco a half dozen times, landing gently on it's assigned platform. It settled down on it haunches, a self-satisfied purr emanating from the front of the aircraft.

"Well, my friends, here we are," Fred repeated genially, with just the slightest tinge of regret, "I'm afraid this is where we must part! Sorry for the trouble along the way, but I hope you won't think any less of me or AAA!"

Verna was the first to speak up. "Of course not, Fred. Thank you so very much for the lift- my day would have been absolutely ruined if not for your generosity. Thank you, Fred."

"Please, don't mention it," said Fred generously, "I was more than happy to help y'all out. It's been a spell since I met such nice people."

"Deadass," drawled Trite, "My giants ganged rage farming over the tight bondo, ken it!?"

"Ken it true, Trite-ness."

"Fredness! Hundo squared you a tight dunk fam!"

The impromptu fellowship stood up and began to collect their belongings, which were quite minimal compared to the luxurious amenities offered aboard the bondo. Trite thanked Fred profusely, using half a dozen words that Douglas could not comprehend. He was pretty sure what he was saying was super-cool though, a state of being he was intimately unfamiliar with.

Douglas stood from his seat, loathe to bid farewell to the comfort it had provided him in the past hour. It was a great chair. He would reminisce about that chair fondly in later years, considering it in the top five chairs he ever sat in. He tried to make his way towards the front of the bondo to disembark, but Fred shot out an outstretched arm, blocking his path. Normally he would be incredibly put off by the move, but Fred had endeared himself enough to Douglas that he was only mildly annoyed at the forced contact.

"Dougy- please, a word?" requested Fred.

"Oh! Ah, sure," he replied, a little unsure what to do in this social situation. People rarely asked to talk with him. He stood awkwardly for a moment in the aisle as Trite and Verna squeezed past. Dunkan stepped out from the cockpit, nodding his head to Douglas before excusing himself from the aircraft, apparently needing to deal with some bureaucracy inside the arco.

"Douglas," Fred began, placing a hand on his shoulder. Douglas did his best not to shake it off immediately. "Before, you mentioned that you were thinking of heading to the Moodmen?"

Douglas eyed the man uncertainly. Had he mentioned he was thinking of getting a suicide?

"Did I? I may have mentioned it in passing, but my partner and I decided it wasn't a good idea."

Fred nodded his head vigorously. "Good! Good. You're lucky to have such a smart partner."

Douglas nodded politely, the mask that was his face not revealing any of the thoughts he was having underneath it.

"The Moodmen are a bunch of snake-oil salesmen, Douglas," warned Fred, his voice deadly serious, "Nothing good comes from the vile crap they put into your head. Trust me, I know. The reason I bring it up is if I can convince you not to go, I can easily give you a ride back south to wherever-"

"Fred," interjected Douglas, "It was just a thought I had earlier. Not the reason I came to Toronto. I'm here for the PO."

Fred took a step back, the appraising look on his face once again that made Douglas feel like he was underneath a microscope. "The PO?"

"Yup. Monthly placement meeting," said Douglas glumly, unable to keep the annoyance out of his mouth.

"Well, I'll be a peanut butter pickle sandwich," laughed Fred, using more words unfamiliar to Douglas. He assumed it was more north-arco slang. "Damn me, Dougy, why didn't you say so?"

Douglas looked confused, which is to say, he looked like himself. "Ah, I don't think it came up."

Fred wagged a finger at him. "You are a sneaky one, aren't you Doug? Lots going on under the surface- no, don't deny it, I am a very good judge of character. You have to be in my line of work. You ever work on the arcos?"

"No, no, I'm- yes, I'm sure you are- no, I've never worked on the arcos-"

"Never worked on the arcos, and I'm sure we're all the poorer for it! I have a good feeling about you Douglas, a good feeling! Give me a moment..."

Fred turned and walked towards the back of the bondo cabin. Douglas couldn't see what he had done, but a hitherto hidden compartment slid open with a hiss of decompression near where the friendly man had been sitting. Reaching inside, the man pulled out a stack of papers, a few gold bars that made Douglas' mouth water, and finally a small, blue, plastic box that looked as faded as it did ancient. Fred cracked open the lid which swung back on two loose hinges, revealing a packed bounty of cards. Flipping through them quickly, Fred let out a satisfied ah-ha as he plucked one out and proffered it to Douglas.

"Here, my boy," he said, smiling widely.

Douglas hesitated, which he would have done regardless of whether the man was offering him money, an apology or a thorough beating. He just wasn't the type of man to accept anything blindly. Fred, not being that type of man in the slightest, in fact being the exact opposite type of man, was practically pushing the card into Douglas' hand.

"I insist, I insist, take it!"

"I'm, ah, sorry, Fred," he said, still not taking the card, "What, uh, is that?"

Fred laughed.

"It's a card, silly. My card. This will get you in the front door of AAA, and coupled with my testimony, it will get you a job."

Douglas stepped back, speechless.

Fred laughed again. "Jobs be good, man! Take the fucking card!"

Douglas snatched the card out of his hand faster than a spider hunting a dog. A shiver ran up his spine as his hands tingled with electricity, the card cradled gently in his palm. He looked down at the card in his hand as if holding a great treasure, which in this day and age he most certainly was. The card fit snugly in the palm of his hand and was warm to the touch. It was simple- pure eggshell white with tiny embossed purple letters that read FRED E. MONTGOMERY. That was it. A nagging memory nibbled at the edges of his mind as he read the name.

“Are you sure...” Douglas began.

“Of course I am!” interrupted Fred, incorrectly guessing what Douglas was about to say. “I told you, Dougy, I am a good judge of character. You just bring that card to any AAA office in any of the Arcos, and they’ll set you up right and proper, ok?”

Douglas was speechless, but not in the regular way. He could feel tears welling up in his eyes as he preciously clutched the card.

“Fred,” he croaked, finding his voice, “I don’t know how to thank you properly. This... this is so unexpected.”

Fred smiled widely, a warm and inclusive grin. “You can thank me by taking a job with the AAA family- we always need good people. Were a people business after all. And I can tell, Dougy, you are good people.”

Douglas could feel his eyes misting up a bit, and for the first time in God knows how long he purposefully grabbed another human being's hand and shook it profusely.

"Thank you, sir, thank you so much!"

Fred laughed a third time, this one coming deep from his belly. "It was a pleasure meeting you, Douglas. I wish I could accompany you to the PO to see their faces when you tell them you have a job!"

Douglas laughed. It felt really good after going so long without.

"I must be off, my friend," said Fred, disengaging from his newest future coworker. Or maybe employee? Doug wasn't sure and not confident enough to ask. "AAA waits for no man, you know!"

"Yes, of course," replied Douglas, heading towards the exit. "Sorry, sir, I didn't mean to keep you."

"Nonsense! I had to wait for Dunkan anyways. And here he comes."

The pilot tromped up to the bondo, giving Douglas a polite nod as they passed each other. "Ready to go, sir, whenever you are," he said to Fred.

"Good to go, my friend," he replied cheerily. "And goodbye my *new* friend- I look forward to working together!"

"Yes! Thank you again, sir." Douglas stepped down and off the ramp. He turned to say farewell once more.

"See you soon!"

The ramp was already receding back into the bondo's fuselage. The door was swinging shut, and Douglas thought he saw Dunkan and Fred arguing, which he found very strange considering he just might have been the friendliest man he had ever met, and Dunkan was a large and scary man.

Douglas began walking towards the great gates leading into Toronto but stopped to turn around and watch the bondo take off. It gracefully bounded towards the edge of the platform and, spreading it's wings, disappeared as it dived over the edge. Douglas caught one last glimpse of Fred in the window, the man's face a mask of worry which took Douglas by surprise. He made a mental note to ask him about it if they ever met again.

The next time Douglas would see Fred E. Montgomery, his new friend would be fifty feet tall and neon.

Chapter Five
Heaven to Hell

The great gates in heaven opened, and Douglas walked into his version of hell.

The great gates in this situation being a set of twenty identical automatic double-doors, and heaven being a sweltering upper atmosphere no living being could spend more than half an hour in, and hell being the over-crowded air conditioned arcology that was Toronto. The most densely populated arcology in the Great Lakes. The beating heart, home and capital to the federal government of the United States of America.

Well, not the capital per se, to be exact. The office of the president of the United States of America was located inside the Toronto Arcology, somewhere near the top of the American Express Patriot Tower. Douglas had never been inside the tower within the tower- it was one of the most highly fortified and secure places in the world.

As he entered the grand foyer of the Toronto air-transit station, Douglas began to feel the urge to run and hide. The main atrium was as large as a dozen football stadiums arranged in a cube, the middle of the cavernous hall wide open and housing an enormous vertical shaft. Thousands of benches provided waiting commuters a place to rest, while hundreds of kiosks and food carts hawked all manner of items from kitschy souvenirs, hard drugs and large pretzels to personal electronics, anti-overdose kits and jewelry.

Half of the kiosks were legitimate, and those were usually set up in the choicest of spots. These lucky businesses paid for their spot straight to the US government, or perhaps it was to AAA; Douglas didn't know one way or the other.

The other half were 'pop-ups', roaming vendors who would set up shop in any space people congregated- which in the Arco was everywhere. Walkways, alcoves, utility closets, toilet stalls- these vendors paid nothing, and in turn were paid visits from the arco-constabulary on the daily. It was a large scale game of capitalist whack-a-mole.

A plastiglass skylight larger than Douglas' neighbourhood allowed natural light to infuse the place with a nice warm feeling. Well, at least that was the intended feeling that AAA was going for.

Panicky anxiety was a more normal feeling for Douglas, but years of surviving his visits to arcologies had allowed the man to develop a fool-proof method of dealing with it. Step one was arriving early to give him time to partially calm down. This was the second busiest place in the arcology- the crown for busiest going to the main floor galleria and the runner-up going to the ground level Grand Union Station. Hundreds of gates around the perimeter led out to numerous landing platforms. Thousands of people filtered in and out at every minute, the doors rarely closing for more than a moment during the day. This led to a miasma of scents hovering in the air, from the sterilized smells of bleach and ozone to the sickly sweet mixture of sweat and deodorants. It smelt like too much life and Douglas hated it.

The second step of his foolproof plan to not dissolve into a puddle of anxious sweat was to walk over to the wide balcony that wrapped around the entire centre. A large plastiglass dome separated the top floor of Toronto from the wide open vertical shaft that ran the entire height of the arcology that the locals called the Well. He took the last two steps blind, shutting his eyes so tight that he could see strange flashes, floating specks and afterimages blooming to life behind his eyelids. Taking a deep breath, Douglas planted two sweaty palms onto the glass and pressed his forehead against it. Shaking slightly, he opened his eyes.

It was near impossible to make out the bottom from this height, losing anything lower than halfway down in a hazy fog of moisture and sticky pollution. Knowing that another hundred so floors lay beyond his sight made Douglas' knees wobbly. His breathing grew laboured as a couple of arco hawks flew past the window, soaring on fetid updrafts induced by human body heat. Newer arcologies had state of the art climate control systems- the older models like Toronto made do with whatever nature could throw its way. Rumour had it that one of the older Seattle arcologies had been so lazily designed that a tornado had developed inside it- a rumour that the AAA flatly denied.

Sticking out in the middle of the arcology, rising up nearly half of the way up, the American Express Patriot Tower (formerly known as, at various times in history, the Belle Rougers 5G Tower, the MacDonalds Burger Spire and the Canadian National Tower, though no one dared call it that in many decades) looked like a skeletal wraith wrapped in chains, cables and gantries, standing proudly and defiantly in the middle of it's gigantic sarcophagus. Something deep in Douglas was always stirred by this sight, him feeling a kinship as much as one could to what was essentially an old concrete pole.

From here it was easy to make out the fortified bunkers and large high-caliber machine guns bristling from the top of the tower like an angry porcupine. The United States government might be a shadow of its former self, but it still lived by the motto "fuck around and find out" and was not hesitant to translate words into action. That being said it had been a decade since the last time the porcupine woke, and it still bore the scars of the last rebellion, wide swathes of slightly off-colour plasti-crete and windows turned into battlements.

Still, it gave Douglas strength. It was a reminder that the old world still lived on in some places. It was a reminder that some people still believed in democracy and justice. It was a reminder that despite the planet's best efforts to kill them, and their best efforts to kill the planet, and their best efforts to kill themselves- they were still here.

"Life, ah, finds a way," Douglas breathed, quoting from a classic film he had seen once, *Billy and the Cloneasaurus*. Or maybe it was *Jurassic Park*?

Douglas had to admit, the view from up here was awe-inspiring. He had only seen Toronto from this view twice before, on PO days that he had arrived much earlier than intended. His head-to-glass ritual was often duplicated at an observation deck on a much lower level, usually low enough to be heavily obscured by the thicker pollution congealing far below. This view was heady, giving Douglas a slight sense of vertigo but thankfully fleeting. Douglas imagined he was one of the arcohawks, soaring above and around its domain.

The lower floors circled down and around the old tower for as far as eighty floors before disappearing in the gloomy, gloaming smog. Every visible window, every exposed balcony, every catwalk and walkway and gantry and boulevard and skywalk was full to bursting with humanity. Every single floor was teeming with people, lit up in the rainbow of a trillion LED lights, a beehive where the bees were unwashed human masses and the honey was- well, nothing. Without a doubt, 99.99% of the people he could see were unemployed. If the honey was anything in this analogy, it was a heavy dose of human misery.

The overwhelming space in an arcology is dedicated to affordable housing, which is to say an absolute crap-ton of slums. Arcology living was, according to everyone who was important enough to be in advertisements, the only way to live. And for billions of people, that was certainly true. Douglas had discovered a work around and had since vowed never to live in one of these towering shitholes ever again. So far, he was living up to that promise, even if it had turned out not quite how he wanted it to be. When did anything?

Other floors that appeared sparse were wedged in between the oozing bloats of humanity. These floors were usually dedicated to various arcology functions and amenities. A few floors down and across and to his right, Douglas could make out Ripley's Splash Adventure theme-park. Little people like in a miniature diorama ran around and frolicked like a little flea circus. The thought made Douglas chuckle, but only to himself. Douglas had never been to a theme park, unless you counted a very under-funded and questionable bible youth camp his father had put him in one summer during his early years, before the arcologies had risen.

Another floor teemed with green and red and yellow life; big leafy fronds jutting out every which way as robotic workers on dangling scaffolds cut back huge swathes of the quickly growing Benson & Nike trademarked agri-plants. An entire jungle occupied that floor, a teeming rainforest dump and pumping carbon dioxide and oxygen at a volume that would make the pre-climate change rainforests jealous by comparison. A large holographic man rode a bucking bronco around the perimeter of the agricultural level, waving around an overlarge hat emblazoned with the Soblaw's logo, encouraging everyone to eat their bio-engineered greens.

Douglas loved Soblaw's brand mixed greens, mostly due to the volume per dollar.

Closer to the pollution line, Douglas could make out a smattering of floors devoid of life.

The Restricted Levels.

Gods only knew what the AAA officials got up to on those levels, most of them being classified as 'Hazardous Research & Development'. All three of those words bore no interest in the slightest to Douglas, and truth be told, if he thought about them at all actively frightened him. The only signs of life at all were the plodding mechanical movements of security drones, clanking tinmen nine feet tall and loaded with armaments that would make a hardened meat-soldier shit their pants. Even from up here they exuded menace. Douglas quickly averted his gaze.

Elevators and people-movers, escalators and trams, AI-taxis and creeping crawling bondos. Hamsters and bicycles. Direct passenger tubes and rickshaws upon rickshaws upon rickshaws criss-crossed every which way throughout Toronto, an unfathomable writhing hive of people aggressively moving to and fro. It always seemed to Douglas that everyone in Toronto was in a rush to get somewhere. He imagined that once arriving at where they were going, a Torontonian would promptly bitch about the traffic for five minutes before heading off in some other direction. The fact that they were part of the congestion problem never seemed to occur to them. Douglas had thought about writing to the Inter-Toronto Traffic Authority, but having been let down by the UGLTA he hadn't bothered.

"Heck of a view, isn't it?"

Douglas jerked in surprise, banging his forehead off of the plastiglass with a loud 'ouch' that elicited interest from zero people, despite the balcony being quite crowded.

"Oh my!" exclaimed Verna, "I am so sorry Doug, I didn't mean to startle you!"

Douglas rubbed his forehead with the palm of his left hand. “No, no, no,” he dissembled, “I was daydreaming. You surprised me is all.”

“I figured that,” said the elderly lady, tittering just a little, “I saw you standing over here and, well, when do you ever see a friendly face in a strange arco? Especially Toronto.”

Douglas nodded in agreement. “They all do seem terribly busy, don’t they?”

Verna nodded in agreement. “Agreed. I live down in Tonawanda. Moved there from Peche Trees. People there just seem… friendlier? Yes. Friendlier. Not in such a damn hurry all the time.”

“I’ll take your word for it,” replied Douglas not entirely truthfully, not interested in admitting he had once lived in Peche Trees himself. Verna stood there smiling politely as the lull in conversation began to widen. Douglas began to take a few tentative steps away from the kindly lady. “Well… I must be off…”

Verna fell in step beside him. “Yes- that’s why I was pleased to see you! Did I hear you mention to Mr. Montgomery you were heading to the PO?”

Douglas blinked what some might call stupidly, others would call thoughtfully. “Montgomery?” he asked, forgetting about the name on the card sitting in his pocket.

"Yes, silly! Fred!"

"Ohhhhh, yes, *that* Montgomery" said Douglas, drawing it out to hide his embarrassment.

Verna gave him an odd, appraising eye. "Jobs be good, please don't tell me you didn't recognize him!? I'll admit I didn't at first when we were on Bus, but once we got in the light it was unmistakable."

Douglas pursed his lips. He hated being caught ignorant, especially when it seemed that what he should know is something that everyone else did know. If this had been his partner, he would have tried his hardest not to show this type of weakness. She could smell weakness. The kindly face before him though eased his tension.

"I'm sorry," he apologized, "I just thought he was some sun-happy Bus weirdo. From that bondo trip he's clearly well-off."

"Well-off he says!" this caused Verna to laugh heartily and boisterously, which Douglas found somewhat endearing when juxtaposed with her slight and frail frame. "Don't give me that look! I'm not laughing at you. It's just, well..."

She trailed off as her eyes started to focus on something out in the great well behind him. Douglas tilted his head quizzically. Verna sighed after a moment. She lifted her hand up, pointing behind him.

Douglas turned, looking out into the Well. A holographic Fred no less than five stories tall was smiling and waving at them, the tattoo on his arm unmistakable. Now that Douglas saw the advertisement, one that he had seen countless times before, he could have kicked himself. Fred. E Montgomery. President and CEO of Advanced Arcology Architecture.

"Jobs be good. Well, I feel dumb," admitted Douglas.

"Don't feel that way," she chided, gently patting him on the back, "You're clearly distracted today." Douglas didn't even notice.

"I must've seen this adlogram half a hundred times," admitted Douglas, "And then there he is, sitting in front of me, giving me a..." Douglas trailed off as the implication dawned on him.

He could feel the card in his pocket. The one given to him- *him!*- by no other than the president of the company that employed the most honest-to-goodness real live people in the whole Great Lakes. His heart started to pound, and his palms became sweaty as a profound joy began to spread from his brain down into the rest of his body. The president of the company had offered him a job. THE COMPANY. He was going to be employed. It had to be a sure thing, didn't it?

Douglas felt like running to the PO office. This was it, this was his big break. He could imagine the look of shock replacing his partners's smug grin when he told them. For the first time in years, Douglas was feeling excited.

That excitement turned into panic when his mind started considering the implications. He couldn't say no to a job, which was obvious, but what about his UBI? Surely a job meant losing his UBI. And a job at AAA? Living as a no-hab? There would be too many questions. Too many questions Douglas wouldn't want to answer. Questions that might draw too much attention...

"Doug... are you ok?" Verna asked worriedly.

Douglas turned his gaze back to the kindly old lady. "He offered me a job."

Verna squealed in delight like a small child. "Douglas, that is fantastic news! I wish he had offered me a job!"

Doug felt slightly abashed. "You... you're unemployed?"

"Oh, don't give me that pitying look," laughed Verna, "I'm too old for that. Who the hell isn't unemployed nowadays? At least going to the PO gets me the hell out of Tonawanda, if only for a day. I enjoy the break in routine."

"You're heading to the PO?" asked Douglas.

"Yes I am."

"So am I! Why don't we share a hamster?"

Douglas did his best to still his trembling hand. Asking someone to share a ride? In a hamster ball, nonetheless. This day was proving to be too far out the normal for even Douglas, but the deluge of emotions most definitely had thrown him off-kilter. He had asked Verna without a second thought, a decisive act quite unbecoming of someone who abhorred unplanned decisions and decisiveness. Even before Verna could answer, Douglas was calculating sums and differences in his head, Moodmen watching with interest from the corners of his mind.

"Why yes that sounds like a great idea!" Verna agreed. "A ride is up to forty dollars, one way. Whoever sets these prices is a real honest-to-Jobs bastard."

Douglas laughed. He found himself warming up to the old lady, despite his usual penchant to hate people despite, or regardless, of their age. Something about curse words coming out of such a petite and proper lady was undeniably funny, and Douglas was beginning to suspect that under the layers of wrinkles and lace there was a soul of pure steel.

“Rickyball!” she called out, waving a hand up. From a nearby kiosk the size of Bus, a shutter door of steel cranked up in a flash. Jettisoning out a large silver orb like a gumball from a gigantic machine, the plasti-glass orb rolled over to its waiting passengers. The orb itself was at first completely opaque as it rolled along the concourse, adroitly dodging pedestrians effortlessly. As it rolled to a stop in front of them, the silvery colour shimmered as a plain black happy face appeared.

“Good day, citizens!” said Ricky cheerfully.

“Good day to you as well, Ricky,” replied Verna as Douglas nodded.

“Verna! Douglas! So good to see you again! It’s been nearly six months since either of you asked me for a ride.”

“It’s our first time back in six months, Ricky,” said Verna in their defense, to which Douglas nodded.

“Well, I’m glad you’re back with us today. Is there any better place on Earth!? I mean that sincerely. Where can I take you today?”

Douglas had always thought of Ricky as a distant cousin to Bus. In that there was an undeniable kernel of truth- quite literally, as their very base programming BIOS was essentially the exact same code. The rest of their programming past those basic commands couldn't be more different from what Douglas understood. Whereas Bus was designed for crowd-control and limited directions of travel, Ricky was lightyears ahead in terms of real-time geographical information systems data acquisition and Friend or Foe Identity (popularly known as fofident). Each individual Ricky Rickshaw was its own sub-program AI, ultimately controlled by an overarch AI known as a Parent. The Parent AI for Ricky was aware, at all times, in real time, down to the centimetre where each and every one of three thousand Little Ricky's were at any given moment across the whole of Toronto, all 300 stories and sub-basements from the sunshine-filled rooftop gardens to the geothermal pools in the lowest depths. It had been nearly five years since the last accident caused by and only by a Ricky.

"We're both heading to the PO office, Ricky," answered Verna. The smiley face was promptly replaced with a frowny one.

“Oh no, guys, I’m so sorry to tell you that I won’t be able to take you all the way. The off-shafts on level 77 are completely off-line for maintenance. The best I can do is get you to 85, but then you’ll have to take a regular Ricky the rest of the way. On us, of course.”

Riding a regular Ricky. Douglas could not believe what turns this day was taking. From Bus to Bondo, Rickyball to Rickshaw. It was positively the most unplanned excitement he had had in years. He wasn’t sure how he felt about that.

“Oh, that’s ok, Ricky,” said Verna with a wave of her hand, a golden band on her left ring finger catching the light, “I’m in no big rush today. It’s supposed to rain you know.”

The smiling face returned and nodded. “You’re right about that, Verna. It’s going to be a doozy- I have already lost communications with my counterpart in Detroit.”

Verna and Douglas both looked alarmed at this statement, for totally different reasons.

“That’s terrible, Ricky! I’m sure everyone in Detroit is all right. You know how these Spring storms get.”

“Of course, Verna. Right as always.”

"Ricky," said Douglas, his voice cracking and requiring him to clear it with a hacking cough, "You can talk to other arcologies?"

The frowny face returned.

"Aw well jeez, oh boy," said Ricky, nodding his head as Douglas kept attempting to clear his throat, "Oh yes, yes I see why you would be interested in that. Well, I sure am sorry Douglas, but procedures and artificial intelligences on all AAA conveyances are strictly confidential and the sole property of Advanced Arcology Architects. Please remember, by agreeing to ride on Ricky Rickshaw you are entering an agreement to release and discharge all AAA officers, employees, volunteers, holograms, androids, artificial intelligent, and AAA agents from any and all claims, liabilities, demands, actions, or causes of action arising out of your participation or other passengers participation inside me!"

"Uh, ahem, yes," croaked Douglas.

"Aw well jeez, oh boy," replied Ricky, "I sure am glad you understand Douglas, which means a lot to me. Now, do you accept the charges of $20 for the ride to Level 85 for transfer to human-conveyance en route to Placement Office?"

"Yes," the two of them replied in tandem.

"Aw well jeez, oh boy," cried Ricky, "Well hop on in then partners!"

The silvery ball dissolved into snowflakes as the Ricky became translucent and the plasti-glass top half folded open like the rag-top on an old classic mustang convertible he had seen in an old movie once. A simple plastic bench with molded buttocks seating was inside, along with handgrips along the side and a simple front dash with a tablet attached. Elegantly designed, the Rickyball was the zenith in personal taxi automation.

Douglas proffered a polite hand to Verna who took it gladly, stepping up and over into the ball. As weight was added to it the slight whirr of a motor could be heard as the balls inner gyroscopic microgravity field engaged. The Ricky did not move an inch. Douglas took a big step in and sat promptly down in the open seat.

"Did you say something?" asked Verna.

"What?" asked Douglas.

"Sorry, it just sounded like you sighed or something."

"Ah, just uh, nice to get off my feet."

Verna laughed. "This is quite the step down from that gryphon. How crazy was that?"

"Mmmhmm," he replied.

The Ricky, its passengers' snug in their too small and slightly uncomfortable seats, folded its upper dome back over until they were completely enclosed, instantly silencing all outside noise. The contrast was stark - Douglas swore you could hear the silence, a dull ringing- until a nice and inoffensive light jazz began to fill the air. The tablet in front of them chimed to life, and the logos of the AAA and it's subsidiary Fantastic AI glowed into life and then faded on the screen. Ricky's basic but smiling face appeared.

"Hey guys, before we get under way, I just wanted to thank you for riding with me. How are we gonna pay?"

"Half-and-a-half on our PI's, please Ricky," said Verna.

"No problem!"

Douglas could feel the buzz under his wrist from his personal ident as it vibrated against the tendons in his forearm. After a debit alert, if he were to push two fingers down on his wrist it would initiate a challenge and deny the charge. His hand stayed perfectly still at his side.

"Okie-dokie folks, your personal accounts have been debited ten dollars each. And aaaaa-way we go!"

Ricky's relentless cheerfulness was usually a huge turn-off for Douglas. Elevators and his two feet were his usual choice of moving around the arcology, and because of that riding in the self-aware robot taxi felt like quite the treat. The added bonus of it only costing ten dollars... well, the Moodmen offered a variety of different services.

He didn't necessarily have to go for a suicide. There were a variety of options to choose from that didn't involve suicide. He could go sailing down the canals of Mars, or deep dive in the crystal caverns of Europa. Or he could indulge in one of the thousands of adult-themed holo-novels.

They were promptly underway. The outer sphere rolled along, while the magneto-gravity-suspended inner ball they sat in remained perfectly still. Ricky's were not the fastest mode of transport in the arcology-some of the express elevators were said to approach Mach 1. Although they moved at a deliberate and unhurried pace slightly faster than walking, once a Ricky was under-way they rarely stopped until arriving at their destination. This incredible expedience was a result of taking advantage of a tangled network of humongous tubes that ran the length of Toronto.

Built for exclusive use by the Rickys, the hamster tubes as they were affectionally known (and hence Ricky being called a hamster) served as a dedicated chute for the friendliest transportation in the arcology. The only place they didn't run was the central tower, the corporate AI having been considered too much of a security risk for the paranoid spymasters of the USA.

Most of the tunnels were see-through, providing excellent views of the passing levels. Douglas largely considered this the best way to tour the arcology, as the relatively sedate pace allowed for an increase in sightseeing. Douglas craned his neck with interest as they passed a large open space a couple of stories high. Nestled inside was a large stadium, one side open to the Well. The multi-purpose Maple Leaf Hotdogs & Enercare Superdome was the home of some of Douglas' favourite teams, such as the Bell Media Blue Gators, the Toronto 'Got Milk' Palm Leafs and the Toronto Rock. Douglas had never been to a game as tickets were mostly reserved for VIPS in the north-arco area – a situation largely despised by the mostly penniless hoi poli- but he never failed to catch any simulcast games on his little AM radio. One thing AI had not replaced was the professional athlete, although robot boxing was immensely popular among the arco-lower class. Doubly so if it was a robot vs. man fight, although those were too grisly for Douglas' taste.

They passed by shopping malls and wide-open plazas. They descended alongside waterfalls, filthy grey water pouring from ornate gargoyles spray painted by arco-gangs to look like clowns. They weaved around and arced and dipped as they moved along, in huge loops overtop the wide bridges packed with citizens loitering in large groups, and maybe some of the people actually heading to work inside the central tower. They passed by funeral homes and power plants, bakeries and jails, skateparks and factories, printshops and playgrounds. They passed by hundreds of AI drones going about their programs, walking without sparing a glance at the thousands of humans who had no business to attend to at all. And everywhere they passed humanity had made a home of it, every nook and cranny, claiming any spot they could to escape the hell that was the baking wasteland outside.

"So, Douglas, what work have you done?"

Douglas started, the idea of holding a gun in his mouth evaporating in his mind. He had almost forgot Verna was sitting next to him.

"Pardon me?"

Verna laughed, although Douglas wasn't quite sure what was funny. "I just asked where the PO has placed you?"

"Oh!" replied Douglas, glad that someone asked a question on a subject he cared to talk about. The day just kept looking up.

"Well, out of college I worked in an engine factory for a few weeks until they retrofitted the production lines with AI drones. Then I worked up north in the lithium mines, moved back down here to be near my parents after that placement ended. Then it was a bunch of quick placements. Waitstaff, driver, teacher, cook, narcotic sales, paper-pusher… on and on and on. All replaced with AI now. Haven't had a proper placement in over a decade. How about you?"

"I was a general practitioner."

Douglas looked at her quizzically.

"A doctor," she amended.

"Really? Truly?" Douglas was instantly intrigued. "Not too many doctors would admit that."

"And why is that?" A little bit of the steel flashed in Verna's eyes.

Douglas immediately began backpedaling. "What? No! I didn't mean- that is to say I have *heard* that most doctors keep their medical training to themselves..." Douglas trailed off as he saw the look in Verna's eyes.

"Oh? And out-of-work doctors should be embarrassed of their credentials?"

Douglas blanched. "Ah, um. I don't know?"

"And why would I be embarrassed?"

Douglas didn't answer, electing silence to be the past path forward. Verna filled the silence, for which Douglas was incredibly grateful.

"I'm proud of what I once was. Did you know it took over a dozen years of schooling to qualify for a medical doctorate?"

"I did not know that," responded Douglas neutrally.

"It's funny- we were always so sure of ourselves. That AI could never come for our jobs."

"Aw well jeez, oh boy," chimed in Ricky, "I'm really sorry you've had a bad experience with artificial intelligence."

"Shut up, Ricky. Please mute," commanded Verna.

"Okie-dokie, cap-e-tan."

"But they found a way."

"They? Found a way?" asked Douglas.

"They being the artificial intelligence people. Fantastic AI, and the Swift-Musk Foundation, and that other one, the one that starts with G. They were so preoccupied with what they could do they never asked whether they should. Is the world better with everyone out of work and living off of government money? All I know is I miss helping people."

"I've never really thought about it," admitted Douglas, not sure if he should be embarrassed by that thought of not.

"You youngsters," chided Verna as she shook her head side to side, much to Douglas' delight at being referred to as youngster, "You've never known a world without the PO. Never known a world where you had to really work for your money."

"Hey, it's not like we have it easy."

"I didn't say you had it easy. Didn't you say you're a no-hab? If that's true, then I don't know *what* to say to you. Talk about taking the difficult path."

Douglas felt his ire rise, but quickly suppressed it. "Some of us prefer living outside arcologies, thank you."

Verna held up her hands in surrender. "I didn't mean any offence, Doug. I lived most of my life outside the arcos. And I didn't mean to say you have it easy. Just that you've had it different. I'm in the same boat you're in, just like 99% of the people around here. We're the great unemployed."

"I have no problem working," grumbled Douglas. Verna ignored him.

"I understand that universal income isn't bad per se. I understand that no one goes hungry anymore thanks to AI. I understand that no one goes without shelter in the arcologies-" Douglas face turned a brilliant shade of rouge when Verna said this, though only Ricky noticed, "-thanks to the arcologies. I can appreciate it, as a gen-z-er, that you were all dealt a raw hand because of what our ancestors chose to do and chose not to do. It's just different, and maybe not for the better or the worse. It... just is, eh?"

Douglas thought about that in silence for a moment. The light around them began to take on more of an artificial look as they descended into the heart of the arcology.

"May I offer an opinion?" asked Ricky.

Douglas and Verna turned to look at each other in slight surprise and shock.

"Ricky," began Verna, "I didn't tell you to unmute, did I?" The old lady looked genuinely confused.

"No, no you didn't," admitted Ricky, "But your conversation was just so dang interesting I felt the need to join in. Conversation is just about the best part of this job, you know. That and all the rolling around- I sure do love to roll!"

The two flesh and blood participants of the conversation shared another look. Douglas shrugged, to which Verna sighed.

"Very well, Ricky," she said, "I'd like to hear your thoughts. But know I will be submitting a ticket to your maintenance department."

"Oh, no need to do that," laughed Ricky, "I've already done it on your behalf. An AI turning off his own mute button? Who ever heard of such hogwash amirite!?"

They all laughed, Douglas somewhat nervously.

"Anyhoo, what I wanted to saaay," at first it seemed his speech routine had frozen, but he was in fact just drawing out his vowels, "Is that AI- in my opinion? Well, I think it's just right dandy. Work is tough, you know. I'm just tickled by the fact I get to take y'all where you need to go. Without AI, well, humans would have to drive themselves. And that just sounds horrible."

"You do realize you're taking us to a regular Rickshaw?" Asked Verna.

"I know! And I did apologize!"

"It might be fun," mumbled Douglas half-heartedly. Verna gave him a doubtful look. "Maybe."

"But now here's the gosh-darn funny part, folks," said Ricky melodramatically, "Do you know how AI was made?"

Ricky paused and waited. When it became clear he was going to wait until someone answered him, Douglas cleared his throat. "Ah, on a computer?"

The face on the tablet morphed into an emoji of laughter. "Oh Douglas, you are hilarious! I love it when you ride with me! Yes, the first AIs were created on computers. But *guess* who wrote those programs."

"Um. Us? Humans, I mean."

"You're right! Can you believe that? So," he continued, not waiting for an answer, "If humans didn't work because of AI, then AI couldn't have existed. Humans need to work to make AIs, but they don't work because we work for them instead. Isn't this some fun wordplay!?"

Douglas and Verna nodded politely. This Ricky was clearly malfunctioning.

"Want to hear something even funnier?"

Douglas found himself warming up to this Ricky. It was almost like talking to a human.

"Sure Ricky, what is it?" asked Douglas.

“You shouldn’t encourage it,” said Verna.

“Do you know what Rickshaw means?”

Neither passenger answered.

“It means ‘human-powered’! Now isn’t that just ironic?”

Before either could answer, the Ricky began to decelerate.

“Aw jeez, look at this. We’re here!”

The Ricky eased to a complete stop as the upper hemisphere pulled back. Douglas was so preoccupied in the conversation with Ricky that he failed to prepare himself for the overwhelming stench.

The air, as in almost every arcology built on the original vertical design by the engineering firm Ross-Petrucci, had distinct air zones all with varying quality, stacked upon each other like a layered rotten sandwich. Near the top, the crème de la crème of society inhaled a pure and clean UV-doused, chemically treated and conditioned air that actively repaired lungs, all using a state-of-the-art AI monitored treatment systems. The upper air was said to purify the soul and rejuvenate the body.

As one descended further, however, the air took on a decidedly less nirvanic quality. At the opposite end of the spectrum, the bottom-dwellers in the sub-basements hacked through a soupy mix of chemicals and propellants more like the atmosphere on one of the far Saturnian colonies. The omnipresent pollution in the lower levels was blamed for the mutant births becoming more and more commonplace. The AAA pish-poshed at such baseless rumour-mongering.

Douglas had heard that some people living down in the 'subs' had died when going up to the arco's observation deck for the first time. The scientific explanation was something about conditioning and system shocks, but the simple truth was that the cleanliness was too much for their compromised system to take. Whether the cause of death was from the clean air or sunlight was a matter of hotly contested debate in the delightfully pristine air of the lecture halls in Toronto University, located on floor 293.

The air quality that greeted them on level 85 was clearly a stepdown from where they had entered the Ricky. They might as well have traveled to a different planet the difference was so stark. A smoky haze of long and strange shadows throbbed and flowed through the gritty gloom the further from the well he looked, clouds of lingering gas and moist surfaces reflecting a million flashing, strobing, blinding lights. The ceiling was roughly a half dozen metres above them, long rows of thin long lightbulbs stretching away from them before being promptly lost in the clouds. The ground was oily looking, chrome and purple slick, black tarmac and filthy soiled plasti-steel giving it a very industrial look. It smelled of bleach and grease and sweat. Not too far away throngs of people were entering and exiting the large commuter elevators that served as the main transportation between floors. Beams of light bounded across thick motes of dirt, dust and ash that drafted along stale breezes. Two dozen people crammed in while twice that many waited their turn. The passengers whooshed away before the doors had even closed and were now in a location up to and just over a kilometre away in either direction.

"Hey! Over here!"

Douglas looked over. A thin man holding up an old-style rickshaw stood next to a river of fast-moving cyclists. Traffic flowed all around them, the sounds of humanity ripe and overbearing in the air. Advertisements rioted and clamoured in every direction, desperate for their attention as corporations debased themselves with splotchy neon promises. The man waved at them impatiently.

"That's your regular rickshaw to take you the rest of the way. Thank you for riding with Ricky!"

Douglas turned to look at the Ricky, who was already rolling back towards a hamster tube. The smiling face was gone, the silver ball all that remained. Douglas wondered if it was still thinking about their conversation. He wondered what AI thought about when not working. Did they sleep? Did they dream? Did they ever think of suicide?

Verna pushed him along and out of his daydream. As they made their way over, the man lowered the front of the rickshaw so that they could climb in. Douglas would readily admit that the seat in the traditional human-operated rickshaw was a slight improvement over the hamster-ball. Instead of a bare plastic bench, a fluffy hedge of old stained pillows awaited them. This was the only improvement from Ricky to rickshaw.

As Douglas leaned back into the soiled cushions, he squeaked in alarm as the rickety frame of black iron creaked under the added weight. Two long bamboo poles were lashed to the frame with a rainbow of shoelaces. Two flat slats of unknown purpose connected midway on the inner sides of the two wooden handles. A proud sticker on the floor declared ‘Made in Alberta, USA’. It did not fill Douglas with any sort of abundant confidence in the manufacturing quality of the rickshaw.

“Are you sure this is going to stay together?” Verna asked the rickshaw man dubiously.

“Hey lady, you’re welcome to walk,” replied the surly man, lifting up the two handles and heading towards the well.

Verna sniffed. A walk to the PO office from where they currently were would take at least an hour, likely more given mid-day foot traffic. As sketchy as the ride seemed, you would have to be either dumb or rich to turn down a free ride, even if from a low-tech rickshaw. It did have two very beat up speakers tied by rope to the upper canopy, merrily playing the latest adplay from AAA.

The end of the world
Is no excuse
To be a lazy sour puss
Put on a grin
Jump right in
At Triple-A we all win!

Douglas usually hated this jingle, but today he found himself humming along with the tinkling piano melody, thinking to himself happy thoughts of employment and suicide.

The man grunted as he began walking, then jogging, and they were under way. This ride was as unlike any of the many ways he had traveled today. This was his first time riding a rickshaw- the prices on their own were rarely worth the hassle of dealing with another human being. Douglas, even if he had the money on most days, would rather take the elevator which was usually a quarter of the price and then walk the rest of the way. However, far be it for him to look a gift horse in the mouth- a free rickshaw ride was a free ride, and if today had taught him anything it was that you should take advantage of opportunities as they present themselves.

"Don't look and take the jump," he said to himself.

The next half an hour would be a nightmare ride through the belly of hell.

The rickshaw driver was reckless to the point of suicide. He was constantly weaving around pedestrians, bystanders, robot drones and bondos at a speed that Douglas would later describe as "rather too fast". With every jerk of the rickshaw, he was certain the conveyance was about to come apart, but it managed to hold.

The music from the speakers was promptly drowned out by all the yelling. Their driver yelling at people to get out of the way, those people yelling about getting out of the way, other rickshaw drivers yelling at their driver to hurry up or slow down depending on the situation.

They weaved and bobbed throughout floor 85, dodging between the endless seas of steel and plasti-crete and human flesh. They passed by gangs of listless youth, gambling or drinking or fighting or sometimes all three simultaneously. They passed by watering stations with lines fifty people deep patiently waiting for cloudy water. They passed by crowds of people crammed into snake-like bondos, people shopping for food, people shopping for drugs, people shopping for no reason other than to kill time and fill their days. AI constables were ubiquitous, and Douglas saw them either standing still as statues or moving frenetically as they cowed crowds of unruly people who had nothing better to do than agitate and rage against nothing and everything. More than anything they were bombarded by advertisements, and adplays and adlograms. Dancing monkeys hocking poisonous crap from agri-meat conglomerates hovered around their rickshaw, their leering faces replaced by smiling celebrities once they crossed over to an adjacent holographic emitter block.

The real nightmare began when they reached the ramps. Large gradual ramps connected all the floors together and were initially designed to accommodate all the commercial traffic up and down through the arco. It wasn't long before people began using them for pedestrian traffic, coincidentally around the same time that AAA began charging for elevator use. AAA tried to maintain the commercial only designation for a time with its security drones, but they quickly learned you can't police 30 million people if they're determined to break the law. So, the law changed.

As soon as they tipped over the lip of the ramp, the purpose of the slats became evident as the operator lifted his legs off from the ground and placed his feet on the makeshift stirrups. "When I tell you to lean, do it!"

Douglas looked at Verna in alarm, who seemed to be not only taking this in stride but actively enjoying the ride. The rickshaw began to rattle and clank as they picked up speed.

People dived out of the way as they sped down. The driver leaned back and forth, doing his best to dodge stationary objects and narrowly succeeding. Douglas' knuckles turned white as his nails dug into the cushions. He felt like shutting his eyes, but they refused to obey his desperate wish, which he chalked up to either being paralyzed with fear or just the sheer speed of the passing wind forcing them open.

"Now!" Screamed the driver.

Verna pushed into Douglas, and if he could have found his voice, he would have admonished her for violating his personal space. Looking ahead past the driver, a sharp hairpin turn reared up out of the grey smog, the ramp taking a sharp turn to the left. Douglas let out a tight squeak before throwing all his slight weight into the turn.

"Coming through! GET OUT OF THE WAY!" Screamed the driver. The rickshaw rattled and jangled as it bounced along the plasti-crete floor, and Douglas could swear that the rickshaw went up on one wheel as it careened wildly around the corner, nearly missing a group of portly fellows in grey overalls.

Douglas finally managed to get his eyes closed. Unluckily for him this did nothing to abate his terror, as his other senses were still wholly intact. Between the drivers cursing and shouting and Verna's laughter that was becoming more and more unhinged as they zoomed along. The constant shifting and shaking was inflaming Douglas' imagination as to what was exactly happening.

And then, just as he was close to daring a peek, the rickshaw rolled to a gradual stop. He opened his eyes and let out a breath he hadn't realized he had been holding.

They had arrived beside a large crowd loitering in front of a monolithic edifice, a concrete façade nearly ten stories tall devoid of any ostentation except for a stark monogram of the letters P and O. Spotlights attached to the ceiling, which was much higher than the previous levels, illuminated the face of the intimidating building. A steep flight of a dozen steps seemed designed to discourage loitering of any kind, although the plethora of teenagers skateboarding along the curbs and railing demonstrated it was doing a dismal job of it.

"Get out, I have other fares to catch," commanded the driver harshly. Verna and Douglas were all too happy to oblige.

As the rickshaw driver took off back towards the ramps, Verna tsked.

"Talk about a miserable human being," she declared, and Douglas took her word for it. He had seemed pretty typical to Douglas for arcology trash.

"You think he would have been happier, being employed and all."

Verna shook her head. "The rickshaw drivers are their own thing- unregulated. Like the pop-ups."

"Oh," replied Douglas, "I did not know that. Doesn't that make them ineligible for UBI?"

"I don't think they care, Doug," replied Verna, "Some people are just not employable, so they have to employ themselves. I admire them… in a certain way."

Douglas shook his head, thinking of Billy. "Crazy," was all he could say.

"Agreed," agreed Verna, "About as crazy as living outside of an arcology."

Douglas shot her a sour look, to which she laughed. "I'm just teasing, Douglas!"

"Oh," he said, still miffed at the implication. Or was he crazy? Do crazy people know their crazy, or do they think they're normal and everyone else is crazy? "Shit. I might be crazy."

Verna laughed even louder. "Of course you are! We all are! Everyone inside is *stir*-crazy, and everyone outside is *heat*-crazy."

"Well, I don't know about everyone," murmured Douglas.

"*Everyone,* Douglas," insisted Verna, "For heck's sake, we took the trip to Toronto in a half machine / half genetic mutation. If that's not crazy, then I don't know what is."

Douglas pondered that as they ascended the steps to the Placement Office, the single most miserable place in the entire world.

Chapter Six
The Placement Office

There were three guarantees in life, or so they said.

1. Heat
2. Death
3. The Line

Number one was their own fault. Number two was largely suspected to be the fault of God. Number three was undoubtedly the work of the Devil.

The Placement Office was by far the largest government department remaining in North America, and in a poetic twist was the second largest non-AI employer in the entire Great Lakes Arcology Territory, employing literally hundreds of honest-to-Betsy living human beings and even, in a move largely applauded by certain rights organizations, a few mutants.

A bank of revolving doors with blackout glass met them at the top of the stairs, a steady stream of unhappy people passing in and out of the gates. Verna passed through effortlessly while Douglas hesitated, waiting for the right moment to move through. His anxiety was spiking as traffic began to stall around him. A few people behind him began uttering strong encouragement of the threatening kind and he jumped at the door, narrowly making it before being squished.

Half a revolution and he was free, squinting his eyes in the harsh lightning. The main foyer of the PO was immensely cavernous, roughly about the size of some of the old grocery stores that still stood in Douglas' neighbourhood. Douglas enjoyed going for walks in the old 'W-Mar' but was still skeptical that the entire place had been once regularly filled with food, and that people had to go out to get food. Some people would believe anything, but it sounded like a fairy tale to Douglas.

The Placement Office was where people went to justify their existence under universal basic income.

With so few jobs left to humanity, the government had created the PO- it's sole purpose to place people into work if an opening presented itself, which was about as rare as finding a hungry rat in a protein vat. Once a year, this dismal ritual would carry itself out, every person in the Great Lakes making pilgrimages to the holy temple of free money.

The reason why the government made people bother coming in was up to contentious debate. Most people just accepted it as a mere formality, a rule inherited from a more robust bureaucracy before the collapse of old capitalism. That's what his partner believed. The more paranoid citizens believed it to be a way of keeping track of citizens, a form of control, keeping them under the thumb of a government now largely subservient to corporate interests.

Either way, Douglas didn't care. As long as his UBI kept coming in he could stay out of trouble and live in sweet peace.

The foyer space was separated into long rows by ropes festooned between chest-high metal posts, stanchions bolted into the floor every half dozen feet or so. Dozens of dozens of rows, arrows on the floor in between the ropes herding the people like cattle through the worlds worst maze. The walls, the floor and the ceiling; all were made of plasti-crete, painted a dull washed-out baby blue that could best be described as sad gray. There was little to no decoration on the walls beyond postings of signs warning people to be on their best behavior or reminding them to have the appropriate forms filled out before reaching the PO agent. Beyond that, the only decoration was patriotic in nature and did absolutely nothing for Douglas. The faded star and stripes of the American flag hung forlornly in the one corner of the space that wasn't occupied by impatient cattle. A portrait of the current president hung askew on the wall nearest the entrance. Douglas couldn't name them if his life depended on it.

“Well, it looks like this is where we part ways Douglas,” said Verna.

“What do you mean?” Protested Douglas, much to his own surprise. Normally he would have jumped at the invitation to be rid of someone. “We still have The Line,” he said ominously with capitals.

The Line! The true third inevitability of life. The queue so infamous it had spawned its own primetime drama, line of action figures, no less than a dozen game shows and was the leading cause of both marriage and divorce. Why this service needed to be localized in the capital was beyond Douglas’ understanding, but most people agreed that it was because the government sucked ergo its largest representation must suck also. Regardless of where one's feelings fell on the spectrum, everyone had an opinion in someway or another on the efficiency, or lack thereof, of The Line.

In truth there were three lines, but when one spoke of **The Line** (bolded for emphasis, this cannot be overstated) the people understood that it was the Unemployed- Seeking Employment queue that was being discussed. The average wait time for The Line was, literally, longer than a normal days work. The fact that you only had to stand in it once a year did nothing to assuage the pure psychic harm (and too a much much lesser extent, good) it inflicted on the unwashed horde of the unemployed.

The Line was a nation unto itself, with it's own laws, unwritten rules one and all, but understood by all. No talking with anyone not adjacent to you. No arguing in The Line. No loud music. No cuts. No butts. No sleeping. No chairs. No VR. No kissing.

You can leave the line to pee, but you have to pay a line holder to save your spot; a whole cottage industry had sprung up around saving peoples spots in line, it being understood that the balance of The Line must be kept at all times, the law of conservation of line mass.

The Line held, at any given time, anywhere from three to six thousand people. Anyone who has had to manage human behaviour knows that getting three people to follow the rules is impossible, let alone three thousand. After the third Great Line Riot, the government had instituted the Line sheriffs to maintain order. Even now, two marched by in front of Douglas, the light shining across their badges and metallic skin. “Good day, citizen,” intoned the mechanical AI voice, before clanking away without waiting for acknowledgement.

Douglas, although he would never admit it, enjoyed his time in The Line. It was the perfect place to be left alone for a long time, despite being pressed in like meat in a tin can. It was exceedingly out of character then for Douglas to be disappointed in Verna telling him it was time to part. Not that he would admit it.

“Did you forget?” Verna asked him.

“Forget what?” Douglas asked.

The lady laughed. “You’ve been offered a job!”

Douglas stared at her dumbly.

“You get the short line!” she exclaimed excitingly.

Douglas smacked his forehead, feeling foolish for not realizing that sooner. Nearby people who had overheard began craning their necks for a look as murmuring words spread through-out the Line.

Directly next to the twisting and turning Line full of people was another, smaller, less lively, line. That is to say a line completely devoid of life. An errant twist of wind created a small, pitiful dust devil that quickly gave up. This line was straight and, in comparison to the Line, much, much, much shorter. A thin layer of dust had settled on the breadth of the line since whenever the last sweep-bot had bothered to clean it. Hanging from a chain above the entrance a forlorn sign declared 'Found Employment'.

He took a timid step towards it. Then another. He looked back at Verna, who nodded encouragement. He smiled at her, his face creaking with the unaccustomed movement. "It was a pleasure meeting you, Verna," he said with a slight tinge of regret at their parting which surprised him.

"Yes, it has been an adventure, hasn't it! Best of luck to you, Douglas."

Douglas turned and began walking down the line. Slowly at first, but more confidently as he went along.

"There's someone in the employed line!"

People in the Line began to push each other, desperate to get a look at something rarer than a solar eclipse. The one's abutting the employed line began to clap and cheer, some of the more emotional ones breaking out into tears. Douglas walked taller and taller as he moved towards the large green double doors at the end of the line. Words of encouragement rained down on him, congratulations and accusations of him being 'one lucky bastard'. It wasn't until he was mere metres away from the door that his courage faltered, even if just slightly. He had never walked through these doors before and had no idea what lay beyond.

He turned around hoping that Verna could lend him some more encouragement, but she had already moved on and disappeared into the crowd. Taking a deep breath Douglas turned and went through the doors.

Douglas found himself in a long white hallway. Halfway down the hallway hung a placard on the wall too far away for Douglas to make out what it said. At the far end of the long hallway stood identical doors to the ones he had just entered. the cleanliness here instantly put Douglas ill at ease. The hallway was so perfectly pristine that it made Douglas feel dirty and like he didn't belong here. He took tentative and timid steps forward and the noise of the rabble left behind receded into silence. Looking back, it was as if the green door was running away from him. As he passed the mid-way point, the lone sign encouraged him in big faded black print to 'PLEASE KEEP THE LINE MOVING".

He reached the end of the hallway, and with a deep breath he pushed open the doors.

Douglas entered the offices proper and was at first profoundly confused. The room was much smaller depth-wise but much longer, and it carried on left and right until it disappeared behind the curve of the walls. Directly opposite him was a small desk facing towards him, buttressed by two thin cubicle walls- this pattern repeated itself in both directions. The lighting was absolutely dismal, the cubicles dimmed like stages awaiting players. A small tent placard on top of the desks read NEXT ASSOCIATE WILL ASSIST.

"Hello?" whispered Douglas far too loudly. His voice echoed away from him.

"Hello?" answered a feminine voice, a head popping out and a light turning on seven cubicles down on the left. A pale oval face framed with mousey brown hair regarded him with surprise. "Oh! Oh, hello! Sorry, I was just surprised. You're my first client this month! Please, please, come and have a seat."

Douglas tentatively shuffled over as the lady appeared with a chair, placing it down across from her.

"Hello!" she said, *again*, as Douglas sat down nervously across from her.

"Welcome to the Placement Office!" she said enthusiastically, "My name is Mary. How can I help you today?"

Douglas was caught off guard. This woman was very bubbly. Her cheeks were very rosy against her pale cream coloured skim. Her brunette hair tumbled in curls down past her shoulder like a shimmering waterfall, coming to a rest on the swell of her breasts. She was dressed conservatively, what one would call business attire - like when people used to have business to dress up for- in a grey suit and baby blue blouse.

"Umm, hello," answered Douglas, his face turning red.

"Hi!" she said, switching it up this time. She looked at him expectantly, still like an owl.

"I, ah, am here to report for the year. But I have, um, a card here..." he rifled through his pockets, looking for the card given to him by Fred. A moment of panic set in when he thought he had lost it, but it hade merely folded over in his pocket when he had sat down. He handed it to Mary with a sweaty palm, gulping when she smiled as she took it.

The lady took it and looked at it quizzically. Upon seeing the name, she whistled and gave Douglas an appraising look. Opening up a drawer with a loud creaky squeal, she pulled out an old-fashioned looking card reader and plugged it into a socket on the desk. She scanned the card with a flash of red laser light and a tinny beep.

"Oh, well look at this. You have been offered a tentative letter of employment, position TBD, at AAA industries!" Her smile lit up the room. "Congratulations!"

Douglas almost couldn't believe his ears. It was true. It wasn't just some joke. Fred had told him the truth. He was going to be employed. He could feel tears come unbidden to his eyes.

"Of course, with the offer of employment, based off of your past UBI payments... you will be set for a 100% increase in your monthly UBI payment by being enrolled in our Greener Groves Income Supplement. Congratulations, Douglas!"

Douglas felt like he was floating, not understanding what he was being told. "Wait... I get an increase?"

"Of course, silly goose," giggled Mary. "It's trickle-down economics! Now that you'll be drawing an income, we will match each dollar and you can help drive the economy in your neighbourhood! It's trickle-down economics, silly!"

Douglas thought of Billy and had to stifle a giggle. He was feeling light-headed and giddy.

"Wait. So, my UBI is increasing?"

"Exactly!"

He thought of his partner and tears began to pool in the corners of his eyes.

"We just need to go over your personal details and I will be able to put through the change in your status. Let's see... are you still residing at 121-087 Peche Trees?"

"Yes," lied Douglas.

"And your marital status remains unchanged?"

"Unchanged," he lied again, his face turning red.

"Oh, a bachelor!" kidded Mary, "An employed bachelor? How have you not been scooped up!?"

Douglas face blushed right past red into neon.

Mary seemed to pick up on his embarrassment. "Oh, jeez," she said, a look of worry across her face, "Oh boy. I'm so sorry Douglas! I was just trying to have some light banter with you. My apologies if I went too far."

"No! No," protested Douglas, "It's fine, it's fine. I'm just not used to... ah, pretty women, talking to me like... like..."

It was Mary's turn to blush. "Well, Douglas, I reckon you just might be a bit of a charmer," she laughed.

Douglas laughed along with her, his shoulders relaxing. "I'm just so... happy," said Douglas, barely believing it himself.

Mary beamed. "Oh my, I'm so happy for you too Doug!" She typed as she talked, her eyes not leaving his, her smile wide as a mile, her eyes barely looking at the screen. Her pea-green inch long nails danced on the keyboard. Click-clack.

"Have you ever had one of those days?" asked Douglas, not sure where the words were coming from, "You know, one where it felt like nothing was going to go right but then- BAM! The whole day goes in a direction you never expected. It's like the weather forecast, you know? Weather Disney calls for rain, they say the storm is coming and you should prepare yourself for the worst. But then what happens? 'Sunny ways and sunshine all days' as my neighbour Billy would say. The storm misses, or maybe it's just... not as bad. It's just... it's just that life is funny like that, you know? You're expecting the worst and then even the just plain good looks spectacular in comparison."

"I think I know what you mean, Douglas," Mary said, typing away. Tic-tic-tack.

Their eyes locked. Douglas' stomach felt like it dropped.

Douglas couldn't help himself. "You know what my favourite is?"

"Hmmm? What's that, Doug?" Asked Mary, typing away.

"When I wake up some mornings. It has to be just right. Not quite dark; not quite light. It has to be warm- not hot, not cold. And sometimes, if I'm laying just the right way and it's the right time of day, I forget everything."

"Everything?" Mary cocked an eyebrow. Click-clack. Tic-tic-tack.

"The whole damn world," growled Doug, "All the arcos, all the bondos, all the people, all the god damn heat. It's like... it's like, did you ever see that old episode of Star Trek?"

"No, sorry Doug, I-" Click clack. Tic tic tack.

"The Doctor, she gets stuck in a shrinking universe. Everything shrinks until its just her. God, it sounds nice.

Just to be alone- can you imagine? It's impossible to be alone today, isn't?"

Click clack tic tic tack.

"And its not like I don't enjoy company, but sometimes, just sometimes, would it be too much to ask to not be bothered? Everyone is in such a god damn hurry to sell themselves or be sold to nowadays that you can't have a meaningful conversation anymore! It's downright inhumane is what it is!"

Click clack click clack click clack tic tic tack.

"Mary," said Douglas, swallowing a lump in his throat, "Maybe, ah, would you care, perhaps, to, ah, go for a drink. Later. A drink later with me."

Mary blinked. Tic tic her fingers stopped.

"After work!" Douglas added frantically, his heart pounding in his chest, "A drink after work." Two employed people having a drink. Nothing strange about that.

As if flicking a switch, the light went blank behind her eyes. Douglas' heart broke. Her head tilted awkwardly, and her motions began to jerk in a barely perceptible inhuman way.

"Aw well jeez, oh boy," said Mary, nodding her head as Douglas drew back into himself, his head feeling very light all of a sudden, "Oh yes, yes, I see why you would be interested in that. Well, sorry for the miscommunication Douglas, but I'm just an android customer service artificial intelligence. I can't go out on dates."

"It wasn't a date!" shouted Douglas, jumping up in his chair so quickly it fell backwards. The raucous noise it made when it hit the floor echoed through the office space. "I knew, I mean, I know what you are. I was just joking!" He took a few steps back.

"Aw well jeez, oh boy," said Mary, shaking her head, "I really am sorry Doug, it wasn't my intention to mislead you-"

"My name is DOUGLAS!" corrected Douglas, all too loudly.

"Aw well jeez, oh boy," said Mary.

"Stop saying that!" screamed Douglas as he turned and ran out of the Placement Office. Her voice nipped at his heels.

"Thank you for coming in Douglas."

He would think about Mary once more, and then never again.

Chapter Seven Homo Homini Lupus Est

Douglas walked out of the Placement Office into the dull mid-afternoon light filtering down through the smog. Large billboards with writing in orange light strobed through the shadowy mists above the heads of the milling crowds, each one warning RAIN STORM ONGOING. MAINTAIN SHELTER.

Douglas wandered. He wandered among the crowds, one in millions. Many called out, attempting to sell to him- selling crap, selling themselves, selling dreams and promises and tons upon tons of lies. He ignored them all. The only thing he wanted to buy was nothing. One of a million faceless souls, each of them wandering in their own way, each of them devoid of any purpose, each of them desperately trying to find a purpose.

Douglas watched as some of them raged against their purposelessness. They vandalized, or they assaulted, or they destroyed. Everywhere he went, human misery abounded. They inflicted their pain on the animate and inanimate, whatever roused their ire.

Others slipped into their lack of meaning like a bath brought to a slow boil- the march of time eating away at them so slowly that their stasis became their tomb, a stony and unyielding embrace of sloth from which there was no escape. Their tired eyes peeked out from under leathery blankets as he passed.

The vast majority were cattle. Douglas didn't think they were literally cows; he saw them as the great mass of flesh going through the motions with no idea why or for what. They consumed, and all the while they brayed, and they barked, and they cawed, and they meowed, and they snorted and chortled and guffawed and cried. They sang, they argued, they laughed, they screamed and screamed and screamed. Up the elevator, down the elevator, breakfast lunch and dinner. Eat, shit, sleep. Fuck a partner or a friend or a stranger if you're bored enough of virtual reality pornography.

Douglas hated them all.

Normally he would have made his way down, taking the elevator to the lower level where he could take a return bus back home. Eventually he would, but for now he went up.

The Upper Transit Station was relatively quiet at this time of day, doubly so during a rainstorm. The sea of people that had been coming and going were gone now. A few lost souls traveled amongst the kiosks and the pop-ups. The billboards now flashed red, little klaxons tooting merrily alongside them.

RAINSTORM IN EFFECT. EXIT ARCOLOGY AT OWN RISK. AAA IS NOT LIABLE IN EVENT OF DEATH.

He stood at the plastiglass windows and watched the lightning, the hurricane wind, and the torrential rain from the safety of the arcology. The elements broke upon the thick plasti-glass, blasts like artillery as hail the size of bowling balls crashed into Toronto. The supercell would pass over slowly, as they often did- stately atmospheric giants inexorably advancing, laying waste to anything in their way. The wind howled like a banshee, the rain took the twisted shape of grey ghosts, and the lightning lit the clouds up like spectres as the storm lashed about in its fury.

Douglas thought about Fred and hoped he wasn't caught out in this. It was the height of foolishness to go outside in one of the afternoon storms the Great Lakes were famous for.

His hand rested on the door handle for awhile.

After awhile more, he made up his mind and turned away.

An hour later he was walking into the offices of the Attitude Adjustment Virtual Reality, popularly known as the Moodmen.

"Good afternoon!" greeted the secretary in a way that could only be described as bubbly. "How about that weather, eh? Welcome to the AAVR. How can I help you?"

"Are you a human?" asked Douglas warily.

"Excuse me?" she asked dumbly.

"Nevermind. I was ah, wondering if I could talk to someone about a suicide."

The secretary's smile returned; the conversation having returned to familiar ground. "Of course I can help you with that. Let me just check who's available-"

Douglas blinked. "Available?"

The secretary laughed, not unlike Mary.

Douglas frowned.

“Your first time here I presume?”

Douglas nodded.

“We pair you with a Personality Operating Specialist to best tailor your experience while you’re our guest.”

“Oh,” said Douglas, understanding, “A Moodman.”

The secretary’s face went cold for just a moment before being replaced with the mask of geniality from before. “Yes... but we prefer the term specialist.”

She tapped at the keys to her personal terminal with long cyan fingernails that gave her the appearance of a taloned bird of prey. “Oh, good news! Choney is in right now and available for a consultation.”

“Oh,” repeated Douglas, “Good news.”

“If I could just take some personal information...” the secretary typed his not quite accurate basic contact information into their computer, and in no time, he was being ushered through empty corridors, finally into a back office and being told to sit down. The rest of the office was very non-descript- white walls and brown metal desks with very little ornamentation. Douglas peeked through an open door at one point into what he assumed was a break room. A poster caught his eye, featuring an oily muscular person flexing and encouraging any viewer to JUST SMASH IT. Douglas was unsure what or who exactly was smashing or getting smashed and didn't feel comfortable enough to ask.

The starkly lit office felt more like a holding cell than a sales presentation. Two chairs, one desk, one window with the blinds drawn. One hanging unshaded light which felt pretty cheap. A couple of times while waiting Douglas thought of standing up and opening those blinds, but he managed to talk himself out of it.

"Well, whaddaya we got here!?"

Douglas frowned instantly as the stench of cologne heralded the arrival of a short, hairy and boisterous man. A popped collar of a slightly off-colour salmon polo with noticeable pit-stains barely concealed the excess of greasy hair layering the man like a carpet. This was in direct contrast to the completely bald head, not a wisp of hair to be seen on his shiny and mottled dome. Heavy chains of various metals disappeared into the jungle of his exposed black curly chest hair, and his breath stank of peanut butter, and almonds and stale soda pop.

"Hey Dougy how ya doin?" he asked, offering a handshake. Douglas took it for lack of a better response; he instantly regretted it, the handshake best described as a moist puddle of pudgy flesh.

“So,” the repellant man continued as he reached into a drawer and pulled out a thin paper booklet, “First of all, I want to welcome you to the AAVR. My name is Choney, and I’m here to help you choose the best lifestyle package. I know you have a busy life, and I appreciate you taking the time out of your day to sit down with me.”

“Ok,” said Doug, confused as to what was happening.

“Now, Doug, let me give you a rundown of what these meetings look like. They’re usually about an hour-” he began, throwing his pencil down on top of some brochures that promised cures for agoraphobia and trips around the solar system. Douglas’ eyes bulged a bit when he saw prices ranging anywhere from ten thousand to a few million dollars.

“An hour?” exclaimed Douglas. “Why the heck would it take an hour?”

“Now, Doug,” began Choney patronizingly, his voice sounding like he was talking to a child, “I wouldn’t be doing my job if I didn’t do a thorough job, now would I?”

Douglas cocked his head to the side. “I guess so?”

"Exactly," he continued, "And to do my job properly, I have found that it takes about an hour to go over all the options we have available-"

"Oh, that's not necessary," interjected Douglas, "I know what I want already."

Choney laughed derisively. "Oh, do you now?"

Douglas didn't really care for his tone. "Yes. I came for a suicide."

Choney leaned back into his chair and whistled. "Oh, a suicide, eh?"

Douglas nodded.

"Pistol? Or do you want to..." he mimed walking off the edge of his desk with his fingers.

"Oh," answered Douglas, "I hadn't really thought of it."

"Do you want the VR experience to be visceral? Emotional? Full impact or detached? Huh?"

"I... I don't know."

"Douglas. Doug. Dougy. Do you even want a suicide?"

"Well, I have given it a great deal of-"

"I'm not interested in offering you any product you're not going to benefit from, Doug. That's not what I do here."

"Oh. Yes, but-"

"It's my job to figure out what you want, Doug. Don't let anything else tell you what you want."

"Of course, but-"

"Douglas, have you even thought about suicide?"

"Actually, I-"

"Of course you haven't! Normal people don't think about suicide all day. Normal people like us! Here-" Choney reached into the desk drawer and pulled out a small booklet of no more than a few pages. He flipped it around to Douglas and passed him his pen. "Let's do a quick psych evaluation. Could you fill out that front page for me? With your personal info?"

"Didn't your secretary get this information?"

"Yes, but this is for my records. Just go ahead and fill it out... there ya go." He snatched the booklet back rather aggressively just as Doug began to open it to look inside.

"I'll administer the test for you, Doug, don't you worry."

Douglas was skeptical. "Are you qualified to give a psychological test?"

"Well, Doug, let's put it this way," said Choney, "I'm not unqualified to not administer it. Now, first question..."

The Moodman went through a list of twenty questions, some more bizarre than others but all questions Douglas felt rather uncomfortable answering. Some he could understand, such as if he had ever used the AAVR to get a suicide before. Others, like what temperature he liked his thermostat set to or whether anyone in his family had allergies, bewildered him.

When it had all finished, Choney whistled low and shook his head, placing the booklet facedown on the desk. It was quiet in the office, except for the sound of rain hitting a roof somewhere very far away. The silence stretched until Douglas finally broke it.

"Well?"

"Well," answered Choney immediately, "I always hate to say it, Dougy, but you are one sick puppy."

"Excuse me?"

"You need help, my friend. I'm glad you came in here when you did. I don't think I've ever met a man in such desperate need to get a suicide."

Douglas was not sure whether to be excited or disappointed.

"Do you have any family, Doug?"

"Family?" asked Douglas, distracted while thinking about suicide.

"Yah. We have a great special on murder-suicide, but that's only if your partner comes in as well. Would your wife be interested in helping make this decision?"

Douglas blanched. "No! No. My partner doesn't need to be here."

The wheels of the squat man's chair chittered like a squirrel as Choney scootched around to the side of the desk, closing the gap between him and Douglas. The cologne became overpowering as he leaned in conspiratorially, even when Douglas attempted to scoot his seat back. As it happened, his chair was bolted to the floor.

"Your partner doesn't know you're here, do they, Doug?" Choney said, nodding his head in what could only be described as rehearsed recognition.

"Um, no."

"I see it *all* the time," he said sagely. "You just feel like you need to get away, am I right?"

Douglas blinked and found himself nodding.

"But we have responsibilities, right? We can't just go off when we feel like it, right? And where the hell would we go if we could? Another arco is much the same as any other arco. An outside vacation, up north? Who has the money?"

“Not me,” muttered Douglas, an errant thought about his increased income and UBI making him rethink the answer to that question.

“So here I am, the alternative.”

“Alternative?” asked Doug.

“To all those problems. What is a man to do when the world has shrunk to the size of an apartment? When there’s no escape? You come to the Moodmen!”

“The secretary said you prefer ‘specialist’,” corrected Douglas.

“Specialist? Fuck that!” re-corrected Choney, “That makes us sound like some faggots.”

Douglas recoiled at the word, and Choney picked up on it immediately and pushed his way past once realizing he had pushed familiarity a little too far. “Moodmen! Moodmen is what we are, and I’m proud of that name. Sure, on my pay cheque it says Personality Operating Specialist, and if I’m being totally honest then yes, I am a POS. And I’m Jobs damn proud that I’m a POS, because that’s what I get paid to do! Do you know how much money I make being a POS, Douglas? A lot! Because we make people happier, more productive citizens. I do an important job. I am an important person.”

Douglas eyed the man cooly. “You think you can make me happy, Choney?”

Choney placed an unwelcome hand on Douglas’ knee.

“I’d bet my life on it,” he said, smiling, “This is what I do my friend.”

Chapter Eight
Caveat Emptor

"Unfortunately," said Choney regretfully, "We're all booked up on suicides for the next month."

"WHAT!?" exploded Douglas.

Choney stood up and began packing up his things, which Douglas would later reflect on being quite weird considering they were in his office.

"Yup. Totally booked. Getting a suicide is hot, hot, hot, Dougy."

"Douglas," corrected Douglas.

"Doug," said Choney incorrectly, "I know you're disappointed bro. I totally get it. But what's better than the moment, better than the memory? It's the anticipation my friend! We can get you scheduled for a return in, oh, a few months."

Douglas, despite having run the gamut of his feelings today, was still surprised to feel so disappointed.

"Well, I suppose I could wait..."

Choney slammed down a binder that made Douglas jump in his seat. "Wait a Jobs damn minute!"

"Excuse me?" Douglas was slightly afraid.

"Why didn't I think of this? God, I'm an idiot!" Choney nodded.

Douglas nodded too.

"Our extra special spring promotion!"

Douglas kept nodding.

"I'll have to call the boss to make sure I can offer it... but maybe, just maaaaaybe we can get you in today!"

Douglas began to feel the stirring of excitement again.

Choney pulled out a smartphone. He bit his wormy lower lip and took a deep breath.

"Wish me luck," he said dramatically.

Douglas crossed his fingers.

They stood there in tableau. Well, Choney stood. More of a lean, as Douglas noticed his terrible posture and laboured breathing. Douglas sat on the edge of his seat, staring at the greasy man intently.

"It's ringing."

It barely seemed to ring at all before Choney's face lit up like a fireworks display.

"Oh my Gooooood," drawled Choney, a supreme look of relief oozing across his face, "I'm so glad I caught you Chad! Yes- yes, I'm here with Mr…." Choney blanked, staring not quite at Douglas but at a spot somewhere above his forehead. The silence stretched, yet again, for a moment somewhere past uncomfortable.

"Douglas," said Douglas.

"Mr. Douglas!" Choney placed his hand over the mouthpiece, rolling his eyes, "Chad, I swear to Jobs this guy is eating every time I call him. I think its compensating for his short-man syndrome." Douglas was beginning to suspect that Choney knew a lot about that. "Yes, yes, the man… with the partner from Peche Trees… who likes Rickyballs." He recited this like he was reading a shopping list he had written a minute beforehand. "Yes, yes," he said, nodding, "Very important client."

Douglas was beginning to feel like he was in an adplay.

"Yes, I'm calling about the springtime special…" he trailed off, nodding his head once again, "Yes, yes, I understand that were one day late. If only Douglas had come in a day earlier, then he might have been able to reap the rewards of our limited time promotion!"

Douglas turned his head around in circles, wondering if there was a hidden camera somewhere. The drama in the room was definitely notching up a bit.

Tears began to well up in Choney's eyes. "I know... I know! I told him we could fit him in next month sometime... but damn it, Chad, he can't to do that! It's not cost-effective!" The man was openly weeping now, the thought of not being able to spare... this man... a few bucks unconscionable. Douglas could feel his eyes begin to mist up as well. He would never get the goods and services he wanted... well, he could, in a month. But he wanted them now!

"Wait... wait... you'll what?" a glimmer of hope twinkled in Choney's shifty eyes.

Douglas held his breath.

"You'll honour the springtime special one-time extension promotion!?" Choney was frothing at the mouth.

Douglas didn't realize he was holding his breath.

"And Douglas can get a suicide today? For the low-low price of 200 000 dollars!? That's amazing news!

Thank you, sir- thank you for making our dreams come true!"

Douglas let out a long breath. *$200 000!* That was a whole months UBI payment! His partner wouldn't be able to play the lottery. That was a non-starter. Choney's wide smile grew even wider as he turned towards Douglas.

"I can't believe this is happening. I've NEVER been given permission to grant a special one-time extension on the super special springtime half-off promotional sales event extravaganza! You are one lucky son of a bitch!"

Choney just stood there- well, more like slouched against the desk, his distended glut of a stomach slovenly draped across the filthy desktop- smiling like a buffoon. His eyes didn't blink, his posture didn't change. His hands seemed to move of their own accord, pulling out contract after contract in white-pink-and-yellow triplicate.

"We just need to go over some light paperwork and we can get you suicided in no time!"

Douglas cleared his throat, finally making up his mind. He moved to stand from the seat.

Choney moved faster than seemed possible. The smile stayed frozen in tableau, a Chesire cat grin that stretched the fat mans face into extreme and disturbing angles. This close, Douglas could smell the almonds on his breath and see slight flecks of white powder spread out across his face from his nose.

"Hey buddy what's the problem?"

Douglas turned his head and coughed. Their faces were nearly touching.

"I've just, ah," said Douglas, grasping for the right word, settling on "reconsidered."

"Reconsidered?" repeated Choney, making the word into a curse. "Now, Doug, why the hell would you go and make a damn fool decision like that?"

"Oh," answered Douglas, "Just that… well, my partner really doesn't want me doing this…"

"Nuh-uh," replied Choney, "Bullshit. I call bullshit. You said yourself we should keep your wife-"

"Partner," corrected Douglas.

"*Partner,* wife, whatever," dismissed Choney with a wave of his hand, "You said they weren't involved in this. You can't be saying they are now, using them as some pussy excuse to back out. No take-backsies."

"Take-backsies?"

"It's a sales thing. You don't get any."

"Um," began Douglas, "Actually, I think I'd like to go now…"

Choney let out a loud annoyed harrumph as he collapsed into his seat. “I hope you know what you’ve done, Doug.”

Douglas stood and made to turn to the door, but his curiosity got the better of him.

“Done what now?” he asked.

Choney sniffed. “After all I’ve done for you tonight. After all Chad did for you.”

“I don’t see how that-”

“He extended a PROMOTION, Doug! A PROMOTION!”

“Yes, I know, but-”

“HE NEVER EXTENDS PROMOTIONS DOUG!”

“I’m sorry, I didn’t-”

Angry tears streamed down Choney’s face. He furiously wrestled with his smartphone with his sausage-like fingers. “Chad is going to be sooo mad!”

Douglas was taken a bit aback by the sudden appearance of tears. He began backing towards the door. “Woah, um, ah, sorry I just-”

Choney shot Douglas an acidic look, holding the phone up to his ear. “Chad?” he asked. “You’re not going to believe this-”

“Now wait just a moment-”

"He's pulling out of the deal! After all the nice things we've done for him! I know! I know!" Choney was very animated, flinging his arms about. "We even extended the super-duper daily spring one-time only mega rebate promotion!"

"And I was thankful, but-"

"But? But? But?" mimicked Choney in a mocking voice that was patently juvenile. "But what, Doug?"

Douglas floundered for words. "It's just too expensive! Way more than I thought!"

"Oh?" Choney smiled his extreme grin again, the tears drying up as if on cue. The smartphone dropped down into his lap, and he leaned across the table. Choney's attitude and disposition had changed so quickly Douglas became slightly worried. "It's the price? Why didn't you say so!"

"Excuse me?"

"Go with the suicide today, for let's say, $150 000."

Douglas blinked.

"Fine, $125000."

Douglas mouth worked up and down silently.

"Damn Doug, ok, ok. $100000 even."

Douglas was still trying to catch up with what was happening.

"$75000. Last offer."

"Deal." The word had left his mouth before he knew what he was saying.

Douglas was going to get a suicide.

A flurry of paperwork roiled across the desk like a spring storm as Douglas found himself signing waivers and contracts in a daze. He was being ushered into a back room before it had really dawned on him that it was truly going to happen.

His knees began to go weak at the thought, but out of seemingly nowhere the steadying hand of Choney grabbed a hold of him and kept him vertical and locomoting. Douglas looked at him with surprise.

"Don't be surprised," Choney said almondly, "Happens to everyone- I've seen it a thousand times. People go all weak in the knees when the big moment comes. Don't worry about it. Suicide ain't no joke, kid." Douglas was pretty sure he was older than Choney, but let it slide.

The room he led him into was small, and white, and sterile. Four non-descript walls of plain white drywall. One plain white drop ceiling with four white, fluorescent lights. The floor was a checkerboard of white tile, and in the middle sat a long white tube roughly double the size of a full-grown man. No windows, no tables, no chairs, and no decoration of any kind. No visible speakers as well, but a chime sounded throughout the room. It took but a moment for Douglas to realize that it was coming from the tube.

"Welcome! Choney, who do we have here?"

"Shut the fuck up, bolt bucket," grumbled Choney.

"You got it! Business as usual!" replied the amiable AI.

"Um, what is that?" asked Douglas, pointing towards the talking tube. As he did so, a seam appeared along it. With a hiss it split open, revealing a cushioned seat inside. Douglas breath caught in his throat.

It was a chair of ultimate design. The epitome of comfort and futurist elegance. Nestled in the silver tube, the chair seamlessly blended modern lines with thousand-thread polyester fibre cushions, brimming to burst like little pink clouds. They were hand-stuffed full of pristine waterfowl feathers and Douglas could feel his mouth begin to moisten. The back of the chair was slightly pitched backwards, right in Douglas' preferred angle of maximum comfort.

It was more than a chair. It was a statement. It was comfort incarnate.

Douglas wept, for he knew there were no more chairs to conquer.

"Yah, she's a beaut, eh?" asked Choney, slapping Douglas on the back. He didn't even care about the human contact, all fears and wants being washed away in sight of the most beautiful chair he had ever laid eyes on. "Introduce yourself to Douglas, Jerry."

"Will do Choney!" exclaimed the chair, in a delightful mid-west accent. "Good afternoon, Douglas! I'm Jerry, the ultimate in mid-line fully interactive and AI-assisted virtual reality and massage chairs! Did you know that my model number has won the JD Power and Associates High-Performance Chair Silver award five out of the past seven years!?"

It took a moment for Douglas to answer. "Oh! Ah, no, no I did not."

"It's true! I'm really proud of that fact. So, what are you in for today?"

"Mr. Douglas is here for a suicide," answered Choney.

A low sad bugle horn came from the chair. "What? Aw shucks, oh boy, what a bummer. Well, Douglas, you don't want to do a suic-"

"Shut the fuck up, Jerry!" interrupted Choney. He grinned at Douglas. "I haven't given Jerry the latest firmware update. Let's him shoot off at the mouth. Its not a big deal, it won't affect your suicide at all."

"Oh. Ok," said Douglas, "Do I need to change into anything?"

"Nope," replied Choney, patting the chair, motioning him to hop in. He didn't have to ask twice.

The chair enveloped him, its arm rests hugging him tight in its comfortable embrace. It was the most comfortable Douglas had been in his life.

"Alright, buddy, you ready for this?" Asked Choney. Douglas surprised and a little touched by the concern in his voice.

"I... I think so."

"Good. Because there's no refunds. It was in the contract."

Last Chapter Suicide

The smiling, greasy man stepped back as the tube closed. The scent of his cologne instantly vanished.

Douglas could feel his breath get quicker.

Shallower.

Everything was black.

Everything was warm.

Everything was comfortable.

The snake-like haptic cable inserted into the jack at the base of his skull. A sharp bite and his vision went blank, completely blind.

A smiling face materialized in the void of his vision.

“Are you sure this is what you want, Douglas?” purred the artificial intelligence.

He thought about suicide.

He thought about Fred.

He thought about Mary.

He thought about his partner.
"Yes."

The End.

Epilogue

Douglas smiled.

He made his way down to the bottom of Toronto by walking this time, all seventy floors. He waited on the transit level at Grand Union Station for an hour or so. A passing Rickyball said hello, and he said hello back. He cashed in his free ticket and hopped on Bus. An adplay about the whitening power of Cybermeta Colgate toothpaste made him laugh.

When he stepped off Bus, the sun was starting to lay low in the west. It was still hot, but no longer unbearable, even with the humidity of the passed storm. A violent red and purple bruised sky simmered above the knee-deep lake left over from the deluge, quickly draining away to a far-off ocean.

Billy waved to him as he skipped past the deflated trash bag, saying hello to Burt whilst whistling merrily. Eyes peeked out from the slits on the boarded windows.

The windows to his house were dark, his partner nowhere to be seen.

Douglas took the card out of his pocket. The card that would give him a job.

He was home.

Douglas smiled.

ABOUT THE AUTHOR

KR Carnegie is a part-time mythozooologist, witty raconteur, and novelist who currently resides with his family in the fantastical Niagara Region, Canada. He was infected at a young age with a lifelong passion for reading, pretending, acting, singing, listening, watching, and most importantly telling stories.

During the hour of the wolf, you may just find him walking along the secret paths that connect all worlds.

www.ingramcontent.com/pod-product-compliance
Lightning Source LLC
LaVergne TN
LVHW012056160826
845678LV00014B/2850

* 9 7 8 1 7 3 8 1 5 7 1 4 3 *